Theft of the Sun
& Other New Norse Myths

Theft of the Sun

and Other New Norse Myths

~

written by
Douglas "Dag" Rossman

Foreword by Jodie Forrest

Skandisk, Inc., Bloomington, MN

Skandisk, Inc.
6667 West Old Shakopee Road, Suite 109
Bloomington, Minnesota 55438
www.tomten-skandisk.com

Printed in the United States of America

Library of Congress Cataloging-in-Publication Data

Rossman, Douglas Athon, 1936-
    Theft of the sun, and other new Norse myths / written by
Douglas "Dag" Rossman.
        p. cm.
    ISBN 1-57534-015-1 (alk. paper)
    1. Mythology, Norse--Fiction. 2. Fantasy fiction, American. I. Title.

PS3568.O8479 T48 2001
813'.54--dc21

                                                    2001031376

All of the stories in this collection appeared previously in
various periodicals as follows:

"The Troll Boy," *Mythic Circle* (Vol. 1, 1987); *Viking* (Sept. 1992)
"The Blood-Red Rune," *Mythic Circle* (Vol. 4, 1987)
"Freya's Tears," *Mythic Circle* (Vol. 8, 1989)
"Loki Bound," *Mythic Circle* (Vol 8, 1989)
"The Theft of the Sun," *Mythic Circle* (Vol. 11, 1991)
"Dvalin's Doom," *Mythic Circle* (Vol. 15, 1993)
"Ice-Runes," *Viking* (May 1994); *Berserkgangr* (Vol. 9, 1996)
"The Gift," *Mythic Circle* (Vol. 17, 1994)
"The Kraken Cup," *Mythic Circle* (Vol. 19, 1996)
"The Mark of Nobility," *Viking* (July 1999)

Dedication

For Kjæren, my beloved fangmate
and life's companion

Acknowledgments

First of all, a grateful *tusen takk* to the campers and staff of the Sons of Norway Fifth District Heritage Camp, Fall Creek, Wisconsin, for helping me to hone my story-telling skills, and to the Roke Discussion Group of the Mythopoeic Society, Baton Rouge, Louisiana, for being a pre-submission sounding board for all of the previously published stories. I am especially indebted to Jodie Forrest, M. J. Hooper, and Sharon Rossman, who collectively read all of these stories in their early forms and offered constructive feedback; to Tina Cooper, Denise Logeland, Christine Lowentrout, Lynn Maudlin, and Karin Miller, each of whom served as editor for one or more of the stories that have appeared in magazines; and to Lloyd Alexander, who has been a source of constant encouragement and a wonderful role model.

⌘

Theft of the Sun
and Other New Norse Myths

Foreword

Many readers of *Theft of the Sun and Other New Norse Myths* will first meet their author, Dag Rossman, the way that I first met him: on paper. After he read the opening novel of my Nordic-Celtic historical fantasy trilogy, a lively correspondence sprang up among Dag, his wife Sharon and me. When I learned that Dag wrote short stories based on Norse mythology, I asked him to send them to me. From beginning to end, the material was a delight: drama, myth, epic, humor, parable, all vividly conveyed. It also revealed an astonishing depth of insight into the culture that had produced those myths. I knew that Dag told stories at Nordic festivals, Norwegian-American summer camps and Jungian Society gatherings, but it wasn't until shortly after we'd at last met in person that I realized what a powerful storyteller he truly is.

The occasion was the opening night of my husband Steven's rock opera, "The Rhymer and the Ravens," which was based on the first novel of my trilogy. The Rossmans were traveling from Louisiana, their home at the time, all the way to Wisconsin, and had generously made a detour to North Carolina to visit Steven and me. We were thrilled that Dag had agreed to introduce our show. He looked the part: he wore a red tunic and cape from the period, a bag of Runes at his belt and a circlet on his brow. He carried a staff worthy of a wizard—and carried himself with so much dignity and *gravitas* that an expectant, childlike hush fell over an audience of almost three hundred chattering adults the moment he appeared. After making a graceful speech about the rock opera, Dag promised a sea of entranced faces that they would see Magic done that night. Such was his presence on that stage that they believed him.

The cast, peering wide-eyed from the wings, forgot its stage fright and believed him, too. Dag put a spell on the whole troupe with that speech, and the show was better for it.

In retrospect, I should have suspected what Dag could do. Perhaps he counts a *skald* or two among his ancestors. Skalds, the poets and storytellers of ancient Scandinavia, were respected entertainers whom royalty often hired to chronicle their exploits. Royalty usually treated skalds well, for one's own good name was highly prized among the Norse, and the words of a skald could satirize as well as praise. Words, and those who wielded them, held great power and consequence in Norse society, perhaps all the more so because words were written with the same Runes that were used in divination. The Runes themselves—and therefore our ability to write—were the gift of Odin Allfather. Odin acquired knowledge of the Runes and their magical uses when he hung on the world tree, Yggdrasil, for nine nights in a shamanic initiation. The god of magic, among other things, Odin was the god most preferred by the skalds, who cast spells with words.

As does Dag Rossman. The collection you hold in your hands includes original stories, some retelling of Norse mythology, and some amplification of our under-standing of it as well. That last point is an important and a remarkable one, and I've been privileged to observe it in process. Most writers like to talk shop, and most writers think a fair amount about their work when they're not writing. No exception to these generalities, Dag takes

10 them further still: he studies his material more thoroughly than any writer I have ever met. He ponders his themes. He meditates upon his characters. He contemplates the entire vast and sweeping jigsaw puzzle of ancient Norse cosmology as we currently know it, and mulls over the missing pieces one by one. More than once he's told me, "I think that something we weren't told about happened between this myth and that one, and I want to fill in that blank."

My sense is that Dag holds all of this rich and colorful lore in trust from his forefathers. It is his *wyrd* to tell these tales. Both as a thorough and reflective student of Norse tradition and as a modern myth-maker, Dag has so immersed himself in the wisdom of his ancestors that new depths of it have been revealed to him. We are fortunate to have such a custodian, who doesn't merely narrate these stories: he enriches them.

He'll enrich you, too. Read on, and discover more about Runes and trolls, dragons and Elves, Odin and Loki. Future scholars may well treat Dag Ormseeker, whose acquaintance you are shortly to make, as a Norse Aesop or a Scandinavian Mullah Nasrudin.

Hans Christian Andersen brought Danish folklore into a contemporary mode, made it more accessible, and wrote his own stories using Nordic themes. As you enjoy Dag's tales, you'll realize that he's doing much the same for Norwegian myth and folklore.

Much the same, and more. I promise you, Dag's readers, that you will see Magic done within these pages.

Jodie Forrest
Spring Equinox, 2001
Chapel Hill, NC

Introduction

"All this of the old Norse belief which is flung out for us, in one level of distance in the edda, like a picture painted on the same canvas, does not at all stand so in the reality. It stands rather at all manner of distances and depths, of successive generations since the belief first began. All Scandinavian thinkers, since the first of them, contributed to that Scandinavian system of thought; in ever-new elaboration and addition, it is the combined work of them all."

—Thomas Carlyle, 1840

I loved the Norse myths when I first read them as a youngster . . . and I came to love them even more when, as an adult storyteller, I had the privilege of telling the tales aloud to listeners of all ages. There is a compelling magic about the myths of the Northern gods, their allies, and their enemies, that resonates with some chord deep within the psyche of Nordic peoples, both in Europe and abroad. To listen to these stories is to feel the bracing Northern wind on your face as it sweeps down off a glacier, and to have the hairs on the back of your neck

12 stand on end when you hear the doomsday howl of Fenris Wolf echoing in the night sky. It is not a mythology for the faint of heart.

Most of the surviving stories come down to us from two 13th-Century Icelandic sources, the *Elder* (or *Poetic*) *Edda* and the *Younger* (or *Prose*) *Edda*. The former is a collection of poems composed by a number of different poets, while the latter is a textbook for aspiring poets. The *Prose Edda*'s author, Snorri Sturluson, attempted to weave the contents of those poems—and others he knew—into a cohesive prose narrative. He also explained the meanings of numerous kennings (poetic allusions), and gave mythological examples for them. We can only be eternally grateful to Snorri and the unknown compiler of the *Poetic Edda* for saving all this lore for posterity. But, as was almost surely inevitable when there are so few sources for such an extensive body of myth, the surviving stories leave one wondering "what happened next?" and curious why the various players in the great mythic drama of the North acted as they did.

Having completely immersed myself in the Norse myths in order that I might be able to tell them accurately and effectively, I found that these "loose ends" gnawed at my imagination. Eventually I was compelled to "tie them up" myself by writing a series of new mythic tales, a *New Edda*, so to speak. The first story was written in 1985 (and published early in 1987), the twelfth—and last—one fifteen years later. Most of them are entirely original stories—though firmly rooted in the Nine Worlds of Norse mythology—but even the ones that are essentially retellings of surviving myths explore personalities and motivations in a manner that the original tellings did not.

Two questions are sure to arise: "Does a modern-day

author have any business 'messing about' with old,   **13**
established myths?" and, "In an age of microchips, space
exploration, and unraveling the human genome, are
stories about gods, giants, and dragons even remotely
relevant?" To answer the first question, I will refer the
reader to the quote from Carlyle at the beginning of this
introduction. Think of me as just the latest in a long line
of Scandinavian mythmakers that reaches back at least as
far as the Bronze Age (to judge by the archaeological
record). I have tried to keep my characterizations of
beings and events consistent with what we find in the
Eddas, but—within that constraint—I have followed
wherever my Nordic muse has chosen to lead me.

As for the relevance of ancient mythic symbols to
today's world, the use of parables has always been an
effective, non-confrontational way of getting listeners
first to visualize and then to identify with a particular
problem or situation that they may need to reflect on
and, ultimately, attempt to resolve. In an age such as ours,
when humankind has acquired the almost godlike power
to destroy our world—be it through pollution, radically
altering the global climate, overpopulation, or nuclear
incineration—we may need the metaphors of myth more
than ever before to help us face our own giants and trolls,
both external and internal.

> Douglas "Dag" Rossman
> "Ormsgard"
> Decorah, Iowa
> April 2000

The Ormseeker Cycle

The Nordic skalds—wandering poets and storytellers—were a source not only of entertainment, but also of the latest news and gossip for isolated villages and farmsteads throughout Viking Age Scandinavia. This was also true of its mythic counterpart, the Nine Worlds. Most of the mythic skalds limited their wanderings to Midgard—the world of humankind—but one of them, Dag Ormseeker, roamed throughout the Nine Worlds telling tales and seeking out any he had not heard.

The first three stories in our collection are ones that were told to Dag by his uncle Ragnar Rune-Wise, himself a storyteller and wizard of note. The fourth entry is one of Dag's own tales, perhaps his best known. We are especially fortunate that the parchments bearing each of these first four stories also contain ancillary material that provides glimpses into Dag's own history, which in some ways was as exciting as the stories he told.

The next three stories also have been attributed to Dag; he probably heard "Dvalin's Doom" and "The Blood-Red Rune" while visiting the dwarves in Svartalfheim, and learned of "The Kraken Cup" during his conversations with Heimdall. Dag may or may not have been the original teller of "The Gift," but since it contains a contemporary poem he composed, I have chosen to conclude the Ormseeker Cycle with that story, which has always been one of my favorites.

⌘

Theft of the Sun

It is told that when the renowned skald Dag Ormseeker was but a lad, the compulsion to fly that plagues all swan maidens every ninth year came upon his mother, Hervor, a daughter of King Hlodver. She resisted the restless yearning as best she could, for the last time it had struck it caused her to desert a husband she loved deeply, but the day came when she knew she must fly again or die. So one moonlit night she opened a strangely carved trunk and—half fascinated, half repulsed—lifted out the beautiful swan-skin cloak she had hoped was a thing of the past.

Hervor shook out the cloak and gently straightened a few feathers that were askew. After leaving a letter for her brother Ragnar on her pillow where it would be found in the morning, Hervor slipped out of the hall and hurried to the small lake that lay downslope from the royal manor. Dropping her shift on the shore she waded into the shallows, pulled the feathered cloak about her shoulders, and was abruptly transformed into a lovely swan. For a time the bird swam in graceful circles, looking back at her ancestral home, then with powerful strokes of her wings lifted skyward where she was briefly silhouetted against the moon before disappearing from human sight. Her mournful, buglelike call was both a signal of farewell to the loved ones being left behind and a cry of longing for an old love sought.

Hervor's letter, when her brother found it the next day, was brief and tear-stained. It read:

> *My dear Ragnar . . . forgive me for leaving without a word, but I feared that the family might try to stop me, and the yearning to fly is so over-powering that I have no choice. I know that you thought I'd burned the cloak—as our sister, Hladgud, did when you urged us both so strongly— but it was so beautiful and I thought myself too strong-willed to ever again succumb to its call. Alas, dear wizard, I should have trusted your wisdom in things magical rather than my own.*
>
> *And so I leave our home, and I place my son in your care. 'Twas almost time he was fostered any-way, and I can think of no one I would trust more than you with either his well being or his further upbringing. Please try to explain to him why I had to leave, and assure him of my love. Tell Dag that I go to seek his father . . . which I do. Odin grant that I might find my beloved husband, so some good might yet come out of this terrible curse.*
>
> > *Ever your adoring sister,*
> > *Hervor*

Thus it was that Dag came to be fostered to Ragnar Rune-Wise, a kindly wizard of middling years who traveled widely, hobnobbed with elves, and knew a thing or two about dragons. Small wonder then that the boy was to receive a most unorthodox education—yet one that was to serve him well in years to come.

The first winter of Dag's fostering, his uncle took him along on a Hjultide visit to Ragnar's old friend Yngve Elf-Brow, the king who ruled the Alfmark, a beautiful land of wooded hills, fertile valleys, and tranquil mirrored lakes—now all covered with a blanket of white—that bordered the domain of the Light Elves. Ragnar's promise that Dag might actually meet some of these fabled beings, who usually had nothing to do with humankind, seemed almost too wonderful to be true.

King Yngve's hall was crowded for the festivities on Hjul Eve, and the high-spirited merrymaking promised to last until dawn. Mindful of his young charge's need for a good night's sleep, regardless of the occasion, Ragnar bade their host and the assembled company a reluctant good night and herded Dag out of the hall.

"Well, lad, how did you enjoy the Hjultide celebration tonight? Did you eat your fill?" Ragnar playfully poked his nephew's stomach as they trudged through the snow from the hall to the outbuilding where the king, thoughtful of their privacy, had quartered them.

"Oh, uncle, it was wonderful. And I ate so much I thought I'd burst." The boy chuckled at the thought. "But I've so many questions I wanted to ask you all evening. Mother never would explain anything! Why was that big boar brought into the hall? And why did those men put their hands on its back and make vows to Frey about the great deeds they would do during the coming year?" Dag paused for breath as they reached their quarters, opened the door, and went inside. "And why did they burn the Hjul Log? And, for that matter, I don't understand why this time of the year is called Hjultide anyway. I would think 'Wheeltime' would be in the summer when we can ride wagons, not in the middle of winter when wheels are useless."

As they stomped the snow off their boots, Ragnar held up his hands in mock surrender. "Enough, my boy, enough. You ask more questions than King Gylfi did when he visited Asgard. My poor sister truly did neglect your education, didn't she?" He sighed gently. "Still I know you ask not out of idle curiosity, but from a thirst for knowledge, so I'll answer all your questions. It's a long story—your namesake, Dag Daybringer, is in it, by the way—so you'd better be ready for bed in case you fall asleep before the tale is fully told."

"Oh, uncle, I'd never do that," Dag exclaimed, but, pulling off his boots and outer garments, he slipped beneath the eiderdown comforter and awaited eagerly the weaving of his uncle's tapestry of words.

～

Heimdall, the Watcher, was perhaps the first to notice that something was wrong. Although dawn had broken and Dag Daybringer had long since set out on his journey across the sky vault, his shining-maned horse, Skinfaxi, spreading the light of day in his wake, that light was strangely cold and pale. And there was something odder still—Sol Sun-Maiden, her two horses, and the blazing sun wheel which they drew behind them should have cleared the far horizon by now and begun to warm

20   the eastern lands. But the horses Arvak and Alsvid, their beautiful charioteer, and their precious burden were nowhere to be seen—not even by eyes as sharp as the Watcher's, which could pierce the densest clouds.

Heimdall paced back and forth beside the Rainbow Bridge, perplexed and pondering. Could the giant wolf Skoll, who was forever pursuing Sol, finally have caught and swallowed her? But no, surely ears keen enough to hear the sound of grass growing would have detected Sol's screams of terror, and Heimdall had heard nothing amiss. Still, with each passing minute, he became ever more certain that something dreadful had happened to his kinswoman Sol and her charge. The air was becoming increasingly colder without the sun wheel to warm it, and the atmosphere promised the imminent appearance of snow. If Sol did not resume her daily ride soon, the eternal cold of Fimbul Winter would descend upon the Nine Worlds and many beings could perish.

Heimdall clenched his golden teeth and slowly shook his head. The threat was much too serious for the Watcher to simply remain at his post wondering and worrying, and hoping that one of the other gods would resolve the mystery. No, save for Odin himself, none of the others was as fit for the task as Heimdall—and in a time of crisis it was needful that the Allfather remain in Asgard.

Heimdall turned on his heel and strode back to his fortress home, Himinbjorg, which loomed beside the bridgehead. Hurrying inside he shouted for his steward, an elderly elf who had managed the household affairs at Himinbjorg for many years.

"Stadok, I'm off to Delling's Door to find out what's amiss with my kinswoman Sol and the sun wheel she guides. They seem to have disappeared, and it's getting colder by the minute."

"Oh, d-dear, that d-doesn't sound good," the usually unflappable steward stammered. "I d-do hope you can find them soon, Lord Varvis."

"As do I, old friend, as do I. So tell Vavsun to saddle Gulltopp for me and provision his saddlebags whilst I change into some warmer clothing and strap on my sword."

"And the Gjallarhorn, Lord Varvis? If mischief is afoot, there may be giants on the move." The reliable Stadok's voice was steady now. "'Better prepared and need not, than unprepared and need much' as the saying goes."

Heimdall's golden smile filled the room. "You're right, Stadok, as usual. I'll shrink the horn so I can carry it beneath my cloak." So saying, he hurried off to prepare for his journey.

A short time later, mounted upon his golden-maned steed, Heimdall addressed the fur-clad elf who had held the reins for him. "Vavsun, your eyes are the keenest of a sharp-eyed race, so as I become the Seeker I entrust to you the task of being the Watcher. Should the giants—or any others who might threaten Asgard—approach the Rainbow Bridge, get word to Odin as fast as you can."

Vavsun's eyes gleamed as he responded. "You can rely on me, Lord Varvis. Now fare you well to Delling's Door."

With a wave of his hand, Heimdall wheeled Gulltopp and galloped over the Rainbow Bridge toward Midgard and the portal through which the sun wheel emerged each morning. Though the distance was great, Gulltopp ran like the wind, his mane and that of his

22 unhooded master flowing out behind them. Thus the day was not fully sped ere they came to a halt by Delling's Door, the eastern gateway to the Underworlds.

The intricately carved, rune-bordered portal was closed, but three elves and a taller being stood before the gate apparently trying to determine how to open it. They turned as one when Heimdall rode up and, as he dismounted, the taller being strode toward him, throwing back his hood to reveal the handsome beardless face and golden hair of Frey, the patron god of the elvish race. Though he lacked Heimdall's golden teeth, the smile he flashed was only a whit less dazzling.

"Well met, Heimdall, my dear fellow. I should have known that you'd be along at any minute. You never could just sit at home when there was a mystery to solve or a fair maiden to rescue, eh? Of course not, as my sister, Freyja, has had good reason to appreciate." He released Heimdall's right hand, which he had been vigorously pumping. "Actually, this whole beastly business is more your sort of thing than mine, anyway. I'd rather preside over a rousing fertility rite any day, but you know how the elves feel about the sun—Fair Wheel, they call it—so I felt I'd better come and have a look for myself. I was going to saddle up my horse and come alone, but the elves would-n't hear of it."

Frey brushed the snowflakes from his hair. "So I hitched my great boar, Gullinbursti, to my chariot and brought along as many of the brave lads as could safely fit in . . . wouldn't do to have one of them fall out when we rode through the sky, now would it?" Despite the gravity of the occasion, Frey's eyes twinkled mischievously.

"Seriously though, Heimdall, now that we're here we seem to have run into a problem. There's nothing to be learned out here—no sign of a struggle or anything like that; if there had been the elves would have found it—but the Door is closed and Delling doesn't seem to be at home. At least no one came when I shouted and pounded on the portal." Frey waved his arms in exasperation. "We tried to force it open just before you rode up, but it wouldn't budge. Why don't you have a try at it?" It was snowing much harder now and Frey, shivering a bit, once again pulled the hood up over his head.

Heimdall's brows knitted in an anxious frown. "It gets worse and worse, Frey. Delling wouldn't have left his post willingly—something must have happened to him, too. We *must* get inside!" He strode past the elves, who drew aside respectfully, and—extending his hands toward the door—chanted the runic song by which the dwarf Thjodrörir had first opened the portal long eons past and allowed the sun wheel to set off on its daily rounds. A soaring descant began to issue from the now glowing door, which trembled briefly—then abruptly all sound, light, and movement ceased. There suddenly appeared in the center of the door, throbbing malevolently, a complex design apparently revealed by the music.

Heimdall whistled ruefully. "Now where did that come from?"

"By Father Odin's lost eye," gasped Frey, "what *is* that thing?"

"That, my friend," muttered Heimdall grimly, "is a web of bind runes. They can only be unbound one at a time, and in a particular order. One mistake by the rune-master who tries to unravel that runic knot and he will be instantly obliterated."

The elves looked at each other and shook their heads in dismay as Frey turned to Heimdall. "But could *you* do

24   it? You're not exactly a novice runemaster, you know."

Heimdall reflected a moment before responding. "Yes, given enough time—and I mean days—I probably could. But we don't have that kind of time; the cold is extending its icy grasp much too quickly. There must be another way."

One of the elves, all but his bright eyes and long nose hidden by the high collar of his fur overtunic and the bill of his tasseled cap, stepped forward and asked diffidently, "Excuse me, Lord Varvis, but am I correct in assuming that Delling opens this door each morning by standing in front of it as you did and singing that song?"

"That's right; it's the only way," Heimdall replied.

"Well, then, if the door can only be opened in that manner, how does Delling get outside to sing to it?"

Heimdall pounded his fist in the palm of his other hand. "Of course, you've got it; there has to be another entrance nearby. Now we just have to hope that whoever sealed this door was unaware of it."

Frey enthusiastically clapped the elf on his shoulder. "Oh, well done, Oaivalas, well done. I always knew you were a keen fellow." Then he frowned. "But Thor blast me if I can see another entrance, Heimdall."

"If it were obvious, it wouldn't be a secret entrance, would it?" Heimdall retorted, flashing his golden smile. "I can't see it either, so it must be protected by an illusion of some sort. If it were a temporary illusion the door could resemble anything, but it would be easier to maintain a permanent illusion if the resemblance were to something with which the door shares a similar nature. If the door is wooden, which seems most likely, it surely has retained some bond with the trees from which it was made." Looking rather pleased with himself, Heimdall concluded,

"I suspect that one of these spruce trees that grow amidst the rocks on either side of the gateway is the hidden door. But which one, I wonder?"

His musings were interrupted by an excited interjection from Oaivalas. "Look, Lord Varvis! That third tree to the right of Delling's Door. There isn't any snow settling on its boughs as there is on the others. 'Tisn't natural."

"Not natural, indeed, Oaivalas," Heimdall exclaimed triumphantly. "How can snow settle on an illusion? That has to be Delling's secret entrance. Come on." And, striding to the hillside, he seemed to walk directly into the snowless spruce tree and disappear.

"Njuolgalas, be a good fellow and look after the animals, won't you? Oaivalas and Haksel, you come with me." Snapping these commands, Frey followed Heimdall's example and, with the two elves trailing in his wake, passed through the tree that wasn't there.

Njuolgalas watched them go, then set about leading Frey's boar and Heimdall's horse into the edge of the nearby forest, where they might find at least a little relief from the snow and wind. Having settled the animals as best he could, the elf took shelter beneath the lowermost boughs of a large spruce tree where he wriggled down into the thick layer of dead needles for warmth and began his lonely vigil.

Beyond the secret portal the feeble light of the Underworlds, supplemented by the glowing ball of runelight conjured up by Heimdall, was sufficient for the party to discover that Delling's rooms were vacant, but there was no sign of violence to be seen. The same was true of his son Dag's dwelling, which lay just beyond—but this was not unexpected since daylight had spread across the sky on its accustomed schedule. In fact, Dag and Skinfaxi

26 should be reaching the western portal about now and beginning the shorter return trip home through the Underworlds.

The four hurried on to Sol's hall and there, by the broken stable gate, lay Delling. Of Sol, her horses, and the sun wheel there was no sign.

"By Freyja's golden tears," gasped Frey, "what has happened here? Oaivalas, Haksel—you two have a look around while Heimdall and I see to Delling."

The elves slipped silently away to begin a meticulous search of the buildings and grounds, while Frey joined Heimdall, who knelt by the supine figure of Delling.

"Great news, Frey! He's not dead, just unconscious." Heimdall's fingers gently probed Delling's head and torso. "His pulse is strong, and there are no obvious wounds— not even on his head—yet here he lies, and presumably has done so since this morning. This is very strange, indeed." And Heimdall rocked back onto his heels to consider the matter.

"Wake up, Delling, wake up, won't you. You're our only hope for finding out what has happened to Sol and the sun wheel." Frustrated, Frey shook Delling so hard that his head rocked from side to side. Aghast, Heimdall reached out a restraining hand, but withdrew it quickly when he saw a small black object pop out of Delling's right ear—apparently dislodged by the shaking.

"What's this?" he cried, pouncing on the object like a stooping falcon striking its prey. "By the nine sisters that bore me, it's a sleep thorn. Well done, Frey. Your outburst has served us well. This is one mystery solved, and Delling should come around shortly . . . then, perhaps, we can learn the rest."

True to Heimdall's prediction, it was only a few

moments later when the slightly groggy Delling shook his own head and slowly sat up. As soon as his eyes could focus on Heimdall and Frey—and the two elves, who had just returned—he burst out, "Thank Odin you're here. Something has happened to Sol! We've got to find her." Delling staggered to his feet.

While Heimdall lent him a shoulder for support, Frey exclaimed "But just what did happen to her . . . and to the sun wheel?"

Delling blinked. "I'm not really sure. When she didn't ride through the gateway at the usual time, I came here looking for her." He paused to clear his head. "I didn't see her near the stable, so I went to the door of her hall and called out her name. When she didn't answer, I feared she might be ill, so I went inside—and the whole place was empty. By then I was really beginning to worry, but I thought I'd better check inside the stable just to be sure."

"Yes, yes. Then what?" Frey demanded impatiently.

"I no sooner stuck my head inside than I was grabbed from behind by someone with arms like a pair of iron bands. I struggled as best I could—that's when the gate got broken—but he was too strong, and suddenly I felt a pain in my ear and then I don't remember anything until just now."

"Then you didn't see who held you?" Frey asked in a disappointed voice.

"I was trying too hard to break loose to worry about who it was, Frey." Delling voiced his annoyance at Frey's implied criticism. "But he must have been a giant, judging by the size and strength of his arms."

"Of course," interjected Heimdall. "The giants must have stolen Sol and the sun wheel just after Dag rode off on Skinfaxi or he would have noticed something was wrong. Then they left one or more of their band behind to deal with Delling so he couldn't raise an alarm 'til they were well away. You're fortunate, Delling, that they decided to use a sleep thorn rather than slay you outright. Hmm, interesting." Heimdall mused for a moment before continuing. "My guess is that they used a sleep thorn on Sol, too, or you would have heard her screams . . . and so would I."

"Blast it all, Heimdall," snapped Frey. "I'm not interested in a discourse on their kidnapping techniques—we need to find out where they went and go after them."

"Easier said than done, my testy friend, since we don't know which giants are responsible."

"Excuse us, lords," said Oaivalas quietly, "but I think we may. Haksel has smelt some of the footprints we found—they are those of giants—and he has detected the faint but distinct odor of brimstone! Surely that can only point to the Fire Giants?"

"Are you certain, Haksel?" barked Heimdall. "We don't have time to make a false start."

"You can trust my sniffer, Lord Varvis; it's how I make my living. 'Twas brimstone, right enough. They must have stomped about in it back home in Hillai, the 'land of living embers,' so their boots stink of it."

"Other folk call that place Muspellheim, but the elvish name for it surely is more descriptive," acknowledged Heimdall. "At any rate, Haksel, if you're that certain we are dealing with Fire Giants, then Surt of the Flaming Sword, the lord of Muspellheim, must be behind Sol's abduction. Alas, there is no giant whose power is more to be feared, yet it seems we have no choice but to seek him out in Muspellheim—and that quickly. What think you, Frey?"

"I think it's an awfully good thing I brought along my rune sword, Mistletoe, which slays giants of its own accord. That more than makes up for my not being a brawny fellow like Thor. You know I don't lack the heart for battle, even if it's not my favorite pastime." Frey swept the magic sword from its scabbard and brandished it heroically. "And I vow by the golden bristles of my boar, Gullinbursti, that I'll bring Sol and the sun wheel back from Muspellheim or die in the attempt."

Heimdall clapped his hands in approval. "A noble vow, good Frey, but I hope that we will be able to carry out this rescue without any loss of life."

"That will be up to Surt and his minions; if those scoundrels resist us, I shall have to teach them a lesson they won't soon forget." Turning away from Heimdall, who barely stifled a laugh, Frey began to issue instructions to the others. "Oaivalas, Haksel . . . if you're willing, you may come along with Heimdall and me in the chariot. We're likely to have need of you when we get to Muspellheim." Both elves nodded their approval. "Delling, old fellow, I know you'd like to come along and take a whack at a Fire Giant or two, but you'll have to admit you're not really back to fighting form yet. Besides, we need you to build a huge bonfire outside the gate here to guide us back once we have rescued the sun wheel from Muspellheim. Without a beacon fire, we'd be hard pressed to find our way."

Delling started to protest, then shrugged his shoulders in resignation. "Aye, I'll tend to the fire . . . and I'll try to reassure Dag when he returns. My boy and Sol always travel back here together throughout the Underworlds each night, so he'll be frantic with worry,

30   wondering what has happened to her."

Bidding Delling farewell, the other four hurried outside to rejoin Njuogalas and ready the boar-drawn chariot for its journey. Leaving Njuogalas to assist Delling, they clambered into the chariot, which lurched forward, then mounted steeply into the dark, storm-beleagured sky. The golden glow from Gullinbursti's bristles gave the chariot the appearance of a rising—rather than falling—star.

Gullinbursti's glow was, in fact, the only light that three of the travellers saw until the chariot began to descend toward Muspellheim and they could begin to perceive the eerie red light, pulsating from the mouths of myriad volcanoes, that had enabled the far-sighted Heimdall to direct their course southward.

They landed without too much of a jolt at the edge of the Myrkvid, that great dark forest lying between Muspellheim and the rest of the Nine Worlds. The snow and ice now dominating the more northern lands could not secure a grip here so close to the eternal fires of Muspellheim, whose flickering lights cast bizarre shadows through the outer ranks of trees—ominous, yet possessing a strange beauty. The travelers stood enraptured for a moment, almost forgetting the urgency of their quest.

It was the impetuous Frey who first broke the silence. "Right, then; let's get on with it, shall we? Haksel, you stay here and look after Gullinbursti; Oaivalas, you come along to guard our backs." And throwing back his shoulders, Frey marched boldly into Muspellheim.

Heimdall hurried to catch up with him, and Oaivalas—after pausing only long enough to string his short recurved bow—soon trailed along a dozen paces behind them. In silence the three proceeded deeper and deeper into the Fiery Land, scrambling over and around boulder-sized cinders while taking care to avoid noxious fumaroles, scalding steam vents, and bubbling lava. After a mile or two they came upon a path constructed of volcanic ash, trod flat by generations of giant feet, and decided to follow it to its destination. For miles the path wound its way around volcanic cones, disappearing at last in the gaping mouth of a lava tube on the lower slope of an enormous extinct volcano. Standing by the tube's mouth and leaning on their long, spike-headed clubs were two Fire Giants, each naked save for an oxhide kilt and thick oxhide boots.

"Well, it seems we've come to the right place," mused Heimdall, slowing his pace. Without turning his head, he addressed the elf, who had drawn closer to the two gods. "Oaivalas, I think you'd better take cover before the giants notice there are three of us. When we come out, we may be in a bit of a hurry, and a few well-placed arrows from an unexpected source might slow the pursuit a bit." He and Frey moved slowly to one side of the path, pausing for a moment beside a particularly large block of cinders, to screen the elf's departure.

"I understand, Lord Varvis, and I'll be ready. Good luck." And Oaivalas melted into the landscape, awaiting an opportunity to find a vantage point closer to the tube's mouth.

The two gods resumed their pace and shortly approached the giants, who raised their clubs into the ready position.

"Heer naw, whar do yew fellers tink yeer gawing?" one giant queried, shaking his club menacingly.

"Yar," interposed his partner, "whar?"

Frey drew himself to his full height, and in as haughty a manner as one can assume when speaking to someone who towers over you, addressed the first giant. "We wish to speak to Lord Surt, my good fellow, and we are in a bit of a hurry, so please take us to him at once."

The giants looked at each other and guffawed. "Aw, yar; Sart'll be wantin' ter see yew, too, I'll wadger. Nowt many veesiturs kawm heer, thet's sartin. Foller me." Turning on his heel, the speaker plucked a lighted torch from a crude fixture just inside the entrance and proceeded to lead them up the tunnel formed by the lava tube, his partner remaining behind to guard the entrance.

"What a pair of bumpkins!" Frey whispered to Heimdall.

The tunnel extended all the way into the volcano's crater, where the party emerged to face a magnificent hall of skillfully worked stone.

"Why, this looks like dwarvish craftsmanship," observed Heimdall with surprise.

"Yar," acknowledged their guide, "the leetle peeple halped us. 'Twere thet or be skwayzed, it were. Thay choosed ter halp, thay did. . . after we skwayzed the first un. His leetle eyes popped right outa his leetle haid. Nayver laft so hard in me life." His whole torso convulsed at the memory.

"Utterly barbaric," snarled Frey, placing his hand on his sword hilt.

"Not now," hissed Heimdall, "be patient."

The giant did not seem to notice this exchange and led the gods into the hall. "Veesiturs, Lord Sart," bellowed their guide, and they looked up at the imposing pair that sat in the high seats at the end of the hall—Surt and Sinmara, the ruler of Muspellheim and his consort. They had the thick black hair and swarthy complexion characteristic of Fire Giants, but their bodies were more finely proportioned than those of the tunnel guards, and their faces almost handsome. Surt and Sinmara wore the traditional oxhide kilt and boots, and she also wore a short leather cloak that only partly concealed her ample, yet comely bosom. On the wall behind them, pulsating with an evil red glow, hung Worlds' Bane, Surt's flaming sword.

"Be very careful, Frey," murmured Heimdall. "Don't be misled by the other giants we've met. Surt and his wife are cunning, dangerous adversaries. Don't underestimate them."

Surt's strong, deep voice rang out. "Hrym, you may return to your post." The guide touched his forelock in acknowledgement and ambled off. "Come forward, travellers, and let us have a look at you. It isn't often we get visitors here in Muspellheim. The climate suits us well enough, but most other folk seem to find it a bit too warm for their taste." He chuckled softly. "Though now that the weather farther north seems to be changing a bit, perhaps their appreciation for heat will grow. What do you think?" Surt's saturnine features twisted into a smirk.

"Have done with this cat-and-mouse act, Surt, you villain," shouted Frey, taking a step toward the high seats. "What have you done with Sol and the sun wheel?"

Surt leaped to his feet and towered over them. "Go carefully, Frey . . . yes, I know who you are—and Heimdall, too—there isn't much that I don't know. But I will answer your question because it amuses me to do so, and because there is nothing you can do to change things." He folded his arms and stared disdainfully down at them. "Yes, I took the sun wheel—and the girl, too. And with good reason. Muspellheim is the Fiery Land and we Fire Giants love heat, yet the path of the sun wheel always takes it so far to the north of us that we can scarcely feel its heat and only see its fiery glow low against the northern sky. It wasn't fair that the most ancient of the Nine Worlds should be treated with so little honor, so I decided to remedy the situation." Surt smiled a sinister smile. "Now our honor has been restored and the sun wheel belongs to Muspellheim. Tomorrow we will place it atop this volcano where it will light the Fiery Land forever."

"That remains to be seen, Surt," interjected Heimdall, "but what have you done with my kinswoman Sol?"

"The girl is a kinswoman of yours, Heimdall? That I didn't know. I hadn't planned to bring her back with us, but when I saw her I was quite taken with the beauty of her red-gold hair. I was going to make her my concubine, but Sinmara objected so strongly . . . ."

Surt glanced aside at his wife who, glaring back at him, leaped to her feet and, throwing back her cloak, demanded proudly, "And why shouldn't I have objected? Am I not woman enough for any man?"

While Frey gaped admiringly, Heimdall responded diplomatically "Let there be no doubt on that score, Lady Sinmara, as I'm sure Lord Surt fully appreciates. But wouldn't it contribute to your marital bliss if Frey and I simply removed the source of your annoyance by taking Sol back with us?"

Sinmara rearranged her cloak and looked at Heimdall appraisingly. "You seem to have remarkably good taste—and sense—for someone who isn't a giant, Heimdall. Yes, there is nothing I'd like better than to have that girl as far from Muspellheim as you can take her . . . and the sooner, the better."

"Humph, well, Heimdall," muttered Surt, "since the girl is your kinswoman and you've gone to so much trouble, I think I can afford to be generous and return her to you. She's asleep yet in that bed closet off to your left. Take her and be welcome."

Heimdall strode to the bed-closet at which Surt had pointed and, throwing open the doors, gazed upon Sol's recumbent form. With a cry of relief, he knelt by her side and gently removed the sleep thorn from her ear.

While Heimdall was thus occupied, Frey turned to Surt and demanded "Now, then, Surt, let's have no more nonsense about the sun wheel staying in Muspellheim. Many beings are freezing to death even as we speak, so the sun wheel must resume its daily path as soon as Sol is fit to guide it. You must produce it and Sol's horses *at once*."

"You dare take that tone with me, insolent godling?" Surt snarled. "You have more than outstayed your welcome. Begone at once or taste my flaming sword." And he wrenched Worlds' Bane from the wall.

Mistletoe seemed to leap into Frey's hand of its own accord, gleaming bluish white like glacial ice. "Mistletoe thrives on a diet of giant flesh, Surt, so I fancy she'll be more than a match for your vaunted blade.

The giant leaped down from the dais and launched a vicious overhand swing at Frey's head. Gripping Mistletoe's hilt with both hands, the god managed to parry the blow though the force of it caused him to stumble backwards a pace or two. When the blades met, the air crackled with their unleashed power, and acrid steam billowed toward the ceiling.

Surt stepped back in astonishment. "That's impossible! Your blade should have melted beneath Worlds' Bane's flame."

Frey grinned at him boyishly. "Oh, Mistletoe is special, Surt, very special, indeed. She's the handiwork of a dwarvish master-smith, who forged her in the depths of misty Niflheim. On the verge of the great spring Hvergelmir was she tempered . . . tempered in those icy waters made venomous by the slaver of the dragons that dwell there."

"Dragon venom!" hissed Surt. "Your sword is imbued with the Cold Fire? No wonder it could absorb the flame without being destroyed." He shuddered involuntarily, for dragons were the nemeses of giants and trolls, and there was nothing they feared more. "Still, even if the blades are a match, their wielders are not. I am your superior in reach and strength, Frey, so your doom is inevitable." Surt's eyes gleamed like fire as he leaped to the attack once more, raining blow after blow against Frey's weakening defenses.

With each blow, the earth beneath them groaned and shuddered as if the fabric of the Nine Worlds was being shaken . . . which, indeed, it was, for in order to regenerate the flame that Mistletoe continued to absorb, Worlds' Bane was drawing upon the very energy that binds the Nine Worlds together.

Sensing this—and being concerned for Frey's safety—Heimdall gently but firmly disengaged himself from the grateful embrace of the now revived Sol, and shouted at the combatants to stop . . . but to no avail. Surt was too immersed in battle fury to hear him, and it was all Frey could do to defend himself. Frustrated, Heimdall pulled the diminished Gjallarhorn from beneath his cloak and, murmuring a brief incantation, restored the great horn to its full size, placed the mouthpiece to his lips, and gently blew. Though Heimdall had winded it lightly, the resulting note belled resoundingly through the room, hurling the combatants off their feet and flattening Sinmara against the back of her throne.

"Now that I have your attention, I say enough of this! Frey, surely you can see that you can't defeat Surt. And Surt, you must realize that I won't allow you to kill Frey. If I wind the Gjallarhorn with all my might, your hall will be blown away and the note will echo throughout the Nine Worlds. The hosts of Asgard will march and Ragnarök will be upon us. Are you truly prepared to bring about the Last Battle now?" Heimdall stood poised to lift the Gjallarhorn to his lips once again.

"I will *not* give up the sun wheel," grated Surt.

Frey staggered to his feet, gasping "It'll soon be the end of most of the Nine Worlds anyway if the sun wheel doesn't go back," and he wearily began to raise Mistletoe.

"Will you two headstrong fools never listen? Since neither side can get everything it wants, only a compromise can avoid total disaster for everyone. Here is what I propose: Sol and the sun wheel will return to her home . . . ." Frey grinned and a scowling Surt started to splutter, but Heimdall continued. "Now hear me out, I say. They come back home, but henceforth Sol will alter her route a little each day so that part of the year she will swing closer to Muspellheim—and the other part closer to the northern lands. The folk who live in the North will have to learn to put up with colder, darker winters than before, but ones they can survive . . . and Muspellheim's honor is upheld in the bargain. What say you, Surt?"

A brief period of silence, which seemed to last an eternity, ensued. Finally Surt sighed, "I don't seem to have a great deal of choice, Heimdall, do I, since—as you shrewdly surmised—I'm not really ready for Ragnarök.

38 Let it be as you say . . . but I warn you that your end of the bargain had better be honored or Muspellheim will bring the Last Battle to Asgard."

"You can rely upon my word, and Frey's, too. Can't he, Frey?"

Frey gritted his teeth and muttered his assent though clearly it pained him to do so.

Some time later, after Sol and the sun wheel were aloft and awaiting Frey's boar-drawn chariot to guide them home, Heimdall, Frey, and Oaivalas paused to take leave of the small group of Fire Giants who had escorted them to the border of Muspellheim. The exchange was decidedly cool—not surprising under the circumstances— though in response to Heimdall's query, Surt did tell him that the bind runes on Delling's Door could be destroyed by simply thrusting Mistletoe into the heart of the rune-web and allowing the sword to absorb and dissipate the charm.

The two gods and their elf companion hurried off to find Frey's chariot and its guardian in the fringes of the Myrkvid. On an impulse, Heimdall looked back over his shoulder and, seeing Surt and Sinmara still standing there watching the receding figures of the party from Asgard, he waved them a final farewell.

Surt encircled his wife's shoulders with one arm and raised the other in a reluctant salute. "I hate to admit it, my love, but I could almost like that one—he respects us even though we are the enemies of his race. As for Frey . . . ," Surt's face darkened and his voice thickened, "he and I shall meet again someday, and when we do I vow he won't have that accursed ice-blade to protect him. In fact, by then the gods will have come to hate the very word 'mistletoe.' Just you wait and see."

The giant couple stood in silence until they saw the golden light of Gullinbursti hurtling northward, followed at a distance by the sun wheel; then they turned and, hand-in-hand, slowly followed the ashen path back to their volcanic home.

~

"Well, lad, there it is," concluded Ragnar with a smile. "I think now you can see why this season, when Sol travels closest to Muspellheim, we call 'Wheel Time,' and, of course, we burn the Hjul Log to be sure she can find her way north again."

"Do you think she really needs it, uncle?" queried Dag.

"Well, she's never said, but doing it makes everyone feel better, and it certainly can't hurt because she's come back on schedule every year since."

The boy thought about that for a moment. "I guess that's so. And I can understand now about the vows sworn to Frey on the boar. But why isn't there anything honoring Heimdall?"

The man reached over and rumpled his nephew's hair. "I don't know for certain, but I don't think Heimdall particularly likes to be the center of attention. He freed his kinswoman and the sun wheel without anyone being killed, which is what he set out to do, so I suspect he was happy enough for Frey to get the glory."

The boy absorbed this, nodding briefly, then frowned.

"What's troubling you, Dag? Are you still concerned about Heimdall's honor?" Ragnar asked sympathetically.

"No, uncle, I'm just worried about what Surt said at

40   the end. You know . . . about Mistletoe being cursed or something."

"Then you can put your mind at ease, my boy. Surt forgot that Heimdall could hear every word he uttered, and 'forewarned is forearmed' as they say." Ragnar grinned a toothy grin. "To honor Frey's blade and counter the curse—if there ever was one—they used a powerful runic ritual to change the name of Mistletoe to Protector of Worlds. A very apt name, don't you think? In remembrance of the sword's role in rescuing Sol and the sun wheel, folk hang sprigs of mistletoe in their halls during Hjultide . . . and if a curse was supposed to follow the name, it's awfully hard to imagine it being passed on to such an innocent little plant, now isn't it?"

"Yes, but . . .," Dag began.

"No buts, my boy, no buts. The future holds what it holds for each of us, and there is no point in spoiling the joy of the present by worrying about what may—or may not—come to pass. That's my advice. Now, then, enough tale-telling and advice-giving for one night. It's high time you were asleep. You'll need to be well rested tomorrow if we are going to take a trip by reindeer sled to visit the elves." And Ragnar smiled fondly down at his nephew as he pulled the eiderdown comforter up around his shoulders and tucked him in for the night.

⌘

The Mark of Nobility

The shrill voices of children arguing brought Ragnar Rune-Wise, a wizard of middling years, to the entrance of his tent, a shelter that had been provided for him by the forest elves whose village he was visiting. Sticking his head through the opening, he called out in a calm but far-carrying voice: "Children, children. I can't possibly stay in a trance with you making so much noise. Why can't you play quietly instead of arguing?"

The one human boy in the group, Ragnar's nephew Dag, burst out: "They won't play the games I tell them to, Uncle Ragnar."

"Why should we?" retorted one of the elves, "The majority decided we would rather play something else, and in our tribe the majority rules."

Dag glared at the speaker and then appealed to Ragnar, "But don't they have to do what I say, Uncle? Mother's father is a king, so that makes me a noble." And

42 he tilted his long nose just a little higher toward the sky. The elf children glowered back.

"Oh, you're of royal blood, my boy, no doubt about that. But there is far more to nobility than having royal parentage."

Dag looked puzzled. "I don't understand."

"Well, then, I think it is high time you heard a certain ancient tale from Ormerdal. Come inside the tent and I'll tell it to you." Ragnar turned to the young elves. "You are welcome, too, children, if you wish to join us." They hesitated only a second before following Ragnar and his nephew inside and taking their places on the reindeer skins that lay upon the floor of the tent.

~

One night long, long ago, when Alrek was king in Ormerdal, he had a vision—a vision of the Shining God, Balder the Good, who was beloved of nearly every being in the Nine Worlds. This experience had a profound effect on King Alrek, for he realized that of all the gods, Balder was the gentlest and noblest—yet in all the land he knew of no shrine dedicated to Balder. Such an injustice had to be remedied, and the king wasted no time in having shrines erected in every part of his kingdom and proclaimed that the people must hold special celebrations every year in Balder's honor.

Now, if Alrek had been content to stop with the shrines and ceremonies, all would have been well, for the image of the handsome, good-natured Balder was popular among the people of the kingdom. But the king became more and more obsessed with his Balder cult and, before long, he declared that no other god was worthy of the devotion due the noble Balder. Alrek destroyed the other gods' shrines and ordered that his subjects must no longer hold rituals honoring Odin, Thor, or any of the others.

Well, honoring Balder was one thing, but being forced to abandon the older gods was another, and many in Ormerdal objected loudly. Alrek's response was to send his warriors to the most restless districts where they burned the farmsteads of those who resisted the king's proclamations. Needless to say, it wasn't long before King Alrek had his way—but by then he ruled over a sullen, unhappy kingdom.

It was at that time, as *wyrd* would have it, that one of the greater orms, Girkad Gleaming-Eye, entered the story. Now, you know that the high dragons rarely have anything to do with humans, but perhaps Girkad had eaten some overripe bear meat, or maybe he simply went berserk . . . no one ever knew for sure. At any rate, Girkad began to raid farmsteads throughout Ormerdal, carrying off livestock—and people, too, if they didn't take cover fast enough.

King Alrek sent out his warriors again, this time to hunt for the dragon. But Alrek never led them into the field himself. After all, he reasoned, a king's life was much too precious to risk in such a hazardous venture. Apparently his warriors had similar, if less nobly inspired, thoughts about their own lives—for search as they might, they never seemed able to find Girkad's lair.

Had the king's warriors asked Vikar Tree-Feller, he could have told them where to find Girkad, for the dragon lived in a cave high on the mountain where the woodcutter plied his trade. Vikar was a simple man who lived alone in his cabin in the forest. His only contact with other people was an occasional visit to those who

44   lived on the farmsteads dotting the lower slopes of the mountain. With them he exchanged stories, and traded wood for those few necessities he could not hunt, trap, or gather for himself.

Isolated as they were from the rest of the kingdom, neither Vikar nor his neighbors were aware of the terror that Girkad was inflicting elsewhere for, as yet, the dragon had not assaulted the farmsteads on his own mountain. Thus the mountain farmers assumed that if they did not disturb the dragon, he would not disturb them. An unstated truce with the greater orms had held for so many human generations that no one dreamed there was any reason to be fearful of Girkad.

Some faint recollection of the truce must have been buried in Girkad's crazed mind, too, for he did leave his human neighbors alone for several months. Then during one of his raids, a flight of arrows was shot at him and ripped the membrane of his left wing. The pain blotted out any thoughts except how much he hated all humans. The wounds left his wing sore and made long-distance flying an ordeal, so when next he emerged from his lair, Girkad hunted close to home. The farmsteads on the lower slopes of the mountain provided easy prey for his talons, so he returned time and again. The truce was definitely over!

Vikar was safe from Girkad, because the dragon could not have penetrated the thick forest to reach his cabin. Nonetheless, the woodcutter's heart was moved by the plight of his neighbors, who were in danger of losing their livelihoods—and possibly their lives.

Like the farmers, Vikar was no , but he was extremely strong and could wield an axe like few other men in the kingdom. So one morning, Vikar hefted his long-handled axe over his shoulder and, accompanied only by a brave farmer named Ivar, climbed the mountain until the pines gave way to birches, and the birches gave way to high, bare slopes where there were no trees at all. Stationing Ivar at a safe distance in front of the dragon's cave, Vikar clambered up the rocks until he was perched directly above the opening. At a signal from the woodcutter, Ivar began to shout insults at the dragon.

Very shortly—although it must have seemed like hours to the two men—Girkad poked his head and neck out of the cave to see what was causing such a commotion. So astonished was he at the sight of an unarmed human challenging him, that Girkad hesitated before rushing out to seize Ivar and gobble him up. It was a fatal mistake.

Seeing that the dragon was too far below him to strike with his axe, Vikar leaped onto Girkad's neck and, sitting astride it, buried his axe in the dragon's skull. It was a mortal blow, but the dying dragon thrashed about so violently that Vikar was hurled to the ground. Girkad's venom spattered all over Vikar's lower legs and shriveled them right up to his knees. If Ivar hadn't been there to carry Vikar's pain-wracked body back to his cabin and nurse him through the fever that followed, the woodcutter would surely have perished.

Happily, Vikar did survive. He even fashioned a pair of wooden legs for himself so he could get around on his own, though after what he had done for them, any of Vikar's neighbors would have been proud to take care of him.

As for King Alrek, I wish I could report that he changed his harsh and unreasonable ways and thereafter ruled Ormerdal wisely and well. But the sad truth is that

46 he did not. Thus it was not very long before Alrek's subjects rose up against him, and the crown of Ormerdal passed into abler hands.

~

Ragnar paused, watching the faces of the children, frozen in rapt attention. "So, Dag, which was the greater mark of nobility? Alrek's crown or Vikar's wooden legs?"

The boy blushed. "I guess that noble is as noble does, Uncle Ragnar." Dag turned to the young elves. "I'm sorry I tried to make you do what I wanted. I didn't have any right to act that way, and I hope you'll forgive me."

The elf children grinned and each of them, in turn, clasped Dag's wrists before they all scrambled out of the tent to resume their play. Ragnar smiled approvingly and, as he closed the tent flap and sat down to re-enter his trance, he murmured to himself, "Noble is as noble does, indeed."

⌘

Ice Runes

"Oh, Uncle Ragnar, it was just awful," sobbed the slender lad as he wiped globs of fresh mud from his face. "The village boys were friendly at first, but when they asked about you and I told them that you were the wizard Ragnar Rune-Wise, they became angry. They shouted that the runes were evil and that anyone who used them had to be evil, too. I tried to tell them they were wrong, that I knew you were a good man; but they wouldn't listen and started throwing mud at me. I ran away before they could do anything worse."

"I'm sorry you had to go through that ordeal, Dag, but I am grateful to you for trying to defend my reputation. Unfortunately, children are not the only ones who fear what they don't understand—and such fear often

48   leads to anger and violence."

"But, Uncle Ragnar, they seemed so sure they were right. Is it possible the runes could be evil? Please tell me the truth so I'll know what to believe."

A thoughtful expression furrowed the wizard's brow. "If I tell you what to believe, Dag, it will be my truth and not yours. No, instead, I'm going to tell you two stories about the ice rune . . . and then you can decide for yourself."

The boy looked rather doubtful, but he settled himself on a low chest to listen to his uncle's tales.

~

There was once a beautiful elf-maid named Fawro, who was the pride of her tribe and much beloved by Oavar, one of the bravest of the elves. Hunting in the forests, swimming in the mountain lakes, and telling stories beneath the starry sky, Fawro and Oavar took great joy in each other's company. Alas, their joy was to be short lived. One day while Fawro was swimming alone in the shallows of one of the lakes, Hjaki, a Frost Giant, spotted her as he soared high overhead in his guise as an ice-eagle. Hjaki's frozen heart was melted by Fawro's loveliness, and he decided to have her as his bride. With Hjaki, to think was to act, so he immediately swooped down upon the unsuspecting elf-maid and snatched her up in his talons. Fawro's terrified screams brought Oavar rushing to the lakeshore just in time to see the ice-eagle flying off into the eastern sky with Fawro dangling beneath him.

Hjaki brought Fawro to his home, a glittering palace of ice seated atop a rocky headland jutting out into a sullen, berg-filled sea. He gave her fine furs and rich food, and he tried to do everything he could to please her. Thus Hjaki could not understand why all she did was cry and insist that Oavar would come for her. Had she no appreciation for the cool, regal beauty of ice and for the rugged good looks and awesome power of Hjaki? The answer clearly was "no" and, after a time, Hjaki's thawed heart began to freeze up again.

One morning, Fawro didn't come to breakfast, and Hjaki soon discovered that Oavar had come during the night and stolen her away. The double set of ski tracks leading to the west were a silent testimony to what had taken place. Changing again into an ice-eagle, Hjaki flew off in pursuit of the fugitives.

As soon as Hjaki alit in front of the two elves and transformed back into his giant form, he cast an ice rune on himself so that his body was protected by a flexible armor of ice. Oavar and Fawro loosed arrow after arrow against the giant, but none could reach his flesh. Hjaki reached the couple in just a few of his great strides. Seizing Fawro in one chilly hand and Oavar in the other, the Frost Giant cast yet another ice rune on the elves, encasing each of them from head to toe in clear, glistening ice. Hjaki carried his living statues back to his ice palace by the sea and, as far as I know, there they still stand—waiting for the thaw that will never come.

~

"What a wicked thing to do," gasped Dag. "I guess those boys were right after all—the runes are evil."

"Don't be so quick to judge," cautioned Ragnar. "Listen to the other story, and then make up your mind."

~

Many years ago, when I was just a young wizard and thought I knew far more than I really did, I fell afoul of a most unpleasant minor jarl named Einar Short-Tongue, who had a small holding along the coast. I had been foolish enough to make fun of him in front of his followers, thinking he could do nothing about it because my magic was so powerful. Well, Einar kept his temper, laughed and spoke flattering words to me . . . and plied me with ale. I thought I was "king of the mountain."

The next thing I knew, I woke up from a drunken stupor, chained by my wrists to a huge boulder at the edge of the sea. At first I could not fathom what Einar intended. Then I realized I was sitting on an exposed kelp bed, which meant that the tide was out. Fully alert now, I looked again at the boulder to which I was chained and discovered the high-tide mark was well above any point I could begin to reach. Clearly, Einar expected the incoming tide to drown me!

Now, you might think that it should have been no great thing for a wizard to rid himself of his shackles. But I must remind you that cold iron is proof against many kinds of magic, and it certainly was against any that I knew in those days. So, as the water lapping around my ankles signalled the sea's return, it seemed very likely I would not live to see another dawn. Still, I have never been one to give up easily, so I ran my fingers over the surface of the rock hoping to find a weak spot. At first I could find nothing; then, when I felt around the point where the chain was anchored, I could sense the presence of a tiny crack running back into the rock from the anchoring spike. Quickly I splashed as much water as I could into the crack, then cast the most powerful ice rune spell I could call up on that part of the boulder until, with the sea swirling about my chest, the expanding ice in the crack split the rock wide enough that I could wrench the chain loose from its moorings and stagger out of the sea to freedom. What nature would have accomplished in years, the ice rune did in hours. I was sopping wet, chilled to the bone, and exhausted from using so much magical power . . . but also much wiser.

～

"I'm so glad you escaped, Uncle Ragnar. The ice rune saved you."

"Indeed, it did, Dag." The wizard paused and peered quizzically at his nephew. "Now, tell me, are the runes good or evil?"

The boy hesitated for a moment. "Both, I guess . . . or maybe neither. It wasn't really the ice runes that were good or evil in either story, it was how they were used."

A warm smile spread across the wizard's face. "Exactly, my boy. Good and evil lie in the heart, not in the runes, so be sure of your own intentions should you ever choose to use magic."

⌘

The Troll-Boy

To the small party of travelers, the trail through Myrkdal had seemed the quickest way to reach Sverdfjord and their planned meeting with Einar Sagging-Paunch's dragonship. However, they were overtaken by a violent thunderstorm that soaked them to the bone and threatened to blast them with lightning bolts. They had been forced—and fortunate—to find refuge from the storm at the largest of the farmsteads that clung to the narrow belt of open land lying between the dark forest and even darker lake.

Although unexpected, the visitors had been heartily welcomed by the farmer, and provided with warm blankets to wrap up in while their sopping wet clothes were hung near the firepit to dry. The storm soon rolled on westward past Myrkdal, but since the day was now well advanced and the trail soggy almost to the point of impassability, their host insisted that they stay for supper and a night's rest before resuming their journey. It was an invitation the travelers were quick to accept, especially when they learned that a fellow guest was none other than Dag Ormseeker, the skald who was said to wander throughout the Nine Worlds accompanied only by his elg-hound, Ledgi. There should be some wondrous tales to hear this night if Dag could but be persuaded to tell them!

Much to the travelers' disappointment, however, Dag said nothing at all during the meal, nor later in the evening after the tables had been cleared and the men sat about quaffing good rich ale from their drinking horns. Dag seemed withdrawn and his expression pensive, so none of the visitors felt bold enough to intrude upon his thoughts. Ledgi dozed contentedly at his master's feet, his head resting between his forepaws.

Eventually one of the visitors, Thorstein Ear, apparently feeling the effects of all the ale he had drunk, stumbled to his feet and asked their host where he could find the outhouse.

"It is the last building on the west side of the farmstead, good sir, but I pray you wait a moment until one of the servants can fetch a torch to light your way and an axe to guard you both."

Thorstein peered at the farmer through bleary eyes. "Guard against what, pray tell? I haven't heard any wolves howling this night."

"Not wolves, but trolls are our nighttime bane." The farmer gave an involuntary shudder and, momentarily, his eyes seemed to be focusing elsewhere, as if he were recalling a painful memory. "They don't come often, and they usually don't carry off more than a stray sheep, but I would be a poor host, indeed, to risk a guest's life through carelessness."

"Trolls, eh?" the ale-filled Thorstein belched. "Thor blast their stinking leathery hides! The only good troll is a dead troll!" This declaration met with general, if not unanimous, approval.

"Death to all trolls, is it?" snapped Dag, rousing himself from his evening-long contemplation, and startling the others into momentary silence. Ledgi's ears perked up at the sound of his master's voice.

"Who would argue that trolls have given humankind much reason to love them? Surely not I. But to condemn them all to death out of hand? That strikes me as being a bit too hasty a judgement. Have you never heard the tale of Agnar the Troll-Boy?"

"Never," replied Thorstein eagerly, and he abruptly sat down, his trip to the outhouse forgotten for the time being. "Would you tell it to us?"

~

He was a handsome enough lad, you had to admit. With his long, wart-bejeweled nose, dark leathery skin, broad hunched back, and bent shuffling gait, he appeared to be everything a mother troll could ask for. But, as the old saying goes, "not all is as fair as it seems." Even allowing for his youth, Agnar just didn't fit in—certainly not with his peers, and not even with his family. He refused to take part in such routine pastimes as stealing everything moveable from the human farmsteads in the valleys, tormenting prisoners, and—when nothing better was available—pulling the wings off moths. He even had the audacity to question repeatedly the rightness of these activities.

By the icy bones of Ymir, he might as well have challenged the very meaning of trollhood itself! Which, of course, is exactly what Agnar had done, although he was unaware of it. It was a wonder someone hadn't dropped a boulder on his head to shut him up once and for all.

One day, when a chill wind came shrieking down the cliff face and moaned its message of winter's approach into the mouths of the trolls' caves, the festering wound caused by Agnar's behavior finally broke open. That morning the other young trolls had been poking and pinching a human child that had been snatched away the previous night from a carelessly guarded farmstead. The child's repulsive appearance—its pale skin, thin yellow hair, and faded blue eyes—seemed to demand their abuse. Finally tiring of their sport, the trolls locked the terrified child back in its stout makeshift cage and, yawning and stretching, shuffled off to their rocky beds. Agnar, as usual, had taken no part. In fact, he had hidden himself in a dark crevice where he hoped no one could find him, and he put his fingers in his ears to try to block out the child's screams, but the sound penetrated even there.

After the other trolls had departed and the silence of the cavern was broken only by the sound of sobbing, Agnar crept out of the crevice and slowly approached the cage. As his shadow, cast by the flickering torchlight, fell across the child, it shrieked and scrambled to the other side of the cage.

"Don't hurt me again, oh, please don't hurt me

again," the child whimpered. Its pitiful condition shook Agnar to the very depths of his being.

"Don't be afraid of me. I'm not going to hurt you. I . . . I've come to let you go," Agnar stammered. The decision had come to him suddenly, unbidden, but with an overwhelming sense of rightness about it. Nonetheless, Agnar was not oblivious to the possible consequences for himself, so his hands trembled as he took the key from the ledge and unfastened the lock. The child remained crouched at the back of the cage, for one troll looked very much like another to its human eyes.

"I'm not like the others; really I'm not," said Agnar. "But you're going to have to trust me. I'll lead you to the entrance of the caves so you can get away. No troll will dare set foot outside while the sun is up."

Still the child hesitated, not quite ready to trust its good luck or the earnest young troll that offered it.

"Come on!" insisted Agnar, his voice nearly cracking with stress. "There's no telling when someone might come by. And even if they don't, if you wait much longer to leave you surely won't get home before dark, and the big trolls will be able to catch you again."

That did it. The child emerged from the cage and followed its benefactor, though remaining at a cautious distance. Agnar led the way through a series of winding tunnels, the last one sloping gently upward toward a sunlit entrance. Agnar halted and, before he could say anything, the child darted up the tunnel like a frightened hare pursued by a hungry ferret. The child paused for just a second in the entrance to look back over its shoulder, then disappeared from Agnar's view. Somewhat hurt by the child's apparent ingratitude, Agnar sighed and turned footsteps toward his own family's cave where, if he was fortunate, he might be able to get some sleep before nightfall, the waking hour for trolls, when his deed would be discovered.

Sleep was slow in coming and fitful at best. In the midst of a frightening dream, Agnar was awakened to find himself being roughly shaken by his mother, Ironsnout.

"Now you've really gone and done it, you ungrateful wretch," she shrilled. "It was bad enough that you wouldn't join your playmates in making the little human child squirm and cry. But then you had the nerve to sneak back this morning and turn it loose!" Ironsnout's voice quavered with fury. "You probably even showed it the way out of the caves. There's no use denying it, either. No other troll would have done such a wicked thing." Ironsnout dug her long nails into Agnar's shoulders menacingly. "Well, you'd better hope your father can catch the child tonight before it finds its way home or our family will be disgraced forever. That child was intended for the Troll King's banquet tomorrow night, and he'll never forgive us if he has to go without his favorite dish."

Agnar had never seen his mother so angry, and he was terrified, but he bravely stood his ground. "I don't want to disgrace you and Father, but I'm not sorry I let the child go, and I do hope it gets home safely. It isn't right to torture and eat humans—they have feelings just like us. They're . . . . "

Anything further Agnar would have said was cut short by a tremendous backhand slap from Ironsnout that bounced him off the wall of the cave. "I'll teach you about feelings, you snivelling little human-lover. The next thing you'll be telling me is that humans are people, too."

"But they are," sobbed Agnar, huddled on the floor, "they are."

"What a disgusting lie," snarled Ironsnout, towering over him. "It's clear to me now that you're no troll . . . and never will be. Such a disgrace! Just you wait 'til your father gets home; he'll fix your goose—and it will be no more than you deserve." And with that she stalked out the cave to share her family tragedy with her sister, Stonehead, who lived two caverns down.

Agnar shuddered. Frosttooth in a good mood was none too pleasant to be around; Agnar didn't even want to think about what his father might be like in a rage. Agnar took a deep breath and decided to run away. Clearly he could no longer stay with his parents or, for that matter, with any of the other trolls, yet he would surely be feared and despised by any humans he might encounter—the child had made that plain enough. "Well," he sighed, "I guess it can't be helped. I'll just have to try to avoid both humans and trolls as much as possible." Agnar packed some food and his few special belongings into his birchbark backpack, wrapped his woolen cloak around him, and slipped out onto the moonlit slope that led down and away from the caves.

Hours passed and, as the sky began to turn grey in the east, Agnar started to look for some place to take shelter during daylight. It wouldn't do to be caught out in the open when the sun came up. Agnar had heard scary old trollwive's tales about his people being turned to stone by the rays of the sun. He didn't quite know if he really believed that, but it was certain that sunshine did something awful to trolls and he wasn't about to find out personally just what that something was if he had any choice in the matter.

No caves were to be found in this countryside, and Agnar was beginning to think he would have to take his chances on crawling under a brush pile, when he came to a large clearing in the birch forest and spied a small farm—human by the style of the buildings and the smell that wafted downwind to where he stood just a step inside the margin of the forest. No one stirred yet, but soon they would be coming out to do their early morning chores, so Agnar scuttled across to the storage building, which lay to one side of the other farm buildings. Quickly and quietly he climbed the outside stairs to the loft where, if he could just get inside, he was certain he could find a hiding place among the trunks that are invariably stored in such a place. Agnar cautiously tried the door latch; his luck held—it was unlocked—and he slipped inside.

Just as Agnar was congratulating himself on his success, a low chuckle from the other side of the room told him he was not alone. A very tall, imposing figure with a glowing, golden smile was seated on one of the trunks, watching him. Frozen in his tracks and fighting against panic, Agnar wracked his brain to identify the being. *Not a human surely? No, certainly not with that unearthly smile. Then who . . . or what? Too big by far to be an elf. Oh, no!* Agnar trembled uncontrollably. *It must be one of the Aesir gods. If it's Thor Redbeard I'm doomed; he likes nothing better than smashing in the heads of giants and trolls.* Agnar gulped. *But this one has a yellow beard, so he can't be Thor. Maybe it's Odin Allfather himself; he often wanders about the haunts of humans. No, I see two bright eyes staring at me, not one.* Agnar's brain seemed to be spinning. *Oh, dear, oh, dear, I don't know what to think or what to do— it's been such a horrible night already—I just can't stand any more shocks.*

"Well, now, youngster. If you've finished sizing me

up, suppose you tell me what a young troll is doing hiding on a human farmstead. It's quite the most curious thing I've encountered on this visit to Midgard."

Agnar, his nerves tight as a drumhead and expecting at the least a cuff or a kick, was so startled and relieved at the stranger's kind tone that he dissolved into tears on the spot.

"Oh, come now, trolling. Be still, be still. I'm not Thor, you know. You've nothing to fear from old Rig." And the god flashed his golden teeth, the source of his dazzling smile.

Needing desperately to share his troubles with someone, Agnar poured out his heart to the kindly Rig, finally saying, "And I just can't believe it's right for trolls to be so mean and cruel to humans or to their own kind, for that matter." He sobbed again as he remembered his own plight.

"Of course it's not right, Agnar, but it *is* the nature of trolls to behave that way. It's what makes them trolls, don't you see?"

"But I'm not like that. I don't *want* to be a troll. But how can I be anything else? Oh, dear, what is going to become of me?"

"My boy," said Rig, placing a comforting arm around Agnar's shoulder, "in a world where humans can become more trollish with every selfish, cruel, or thoughtless deed, do you not think a troll can become more human with each generous, compassionate, or thoughtful act? Nothing in the Nine Worlds is beyond redemption, Agnar—certainly not one unhappy young troll. Your heart is already human, and it is with humans you belong."

"I'm human on the inside? How wonderful! I'd

never thought of it that way before." Then Agnar's face fell. "But I'm still a troll on the outside, Rig. Humans will never accept me. They'll always hate and fear me for my appearance."

"Unfortunately, my boy, I'm afraid you are right. Those who get to know you would come to accept you in time, I'm sure, but a hasty axe or arrow might not allow the time to get acquainted. Ordinarily I don't like to do permanent shape changes—it shakes the balance of the Nine Worlds, not to mention giving me a colossal headache—but in this case, since it seems more a matter of righting an imbalance, I'll chance it."

Rig backed away several paces, then stretched both of his arms out toward Agnar and, chanting quietly, began to draw glowing runes in the air between them. For a brief, anxious moment nothing seemed to be happening, then the long trollish nose started to shrink, the leathery skin became soft and pink, and Agnar slowly straightened up to his full height. Standing before Rig was a very ordinary-looking human boy.

"Some transformation runes to give you your true shape and a bind rune to seal it," muttered Rig. "There, that ought to do it. Hmm. Not bad, not bad at all. And not even much of a headache."

"Oh, how can I ever thank you, Rig? You've saved my life . . . and more."

"You can thank me, Agnar, by being the best human you possibly can—nothing more, nothing less. And always remember that the line between human and troll is perilously thin. Now go out and introduce yourself to your new friends."

Agnar started toward the door, then hesitated. "Will I ever see you again?"

Theft of the Sun

Rig flashed his golden smile. "I visit Midgard every now and again—I'm very fond of humans—so you can be sure that I'll look in on you from time to time. Now go!"

Agnar threw open the door and stepped out to face the glorious rising sun, which he would never have to fear again.

~

"An interesting yarn," sniffed Thorstein, "if a bit unlikely. What is supposed to have become of this Agnar fellow afterwards?"

"Why, whatever *could* happen to an unlikely person from an unlikely story?" retorted Dag, bristling at Thorstein's implied disbelief. "I should think he would have grown up and tried his hand at farming like many another man, or does that seem unlikely, too? Never mind; the tale is told and you must make of it what you will. As for me, I must get to my bed if our host will light me to the storehouse. Goodnight, all."

Dag and the farmer left the hall and walked slowly to the storehouse, Ledgi bounding in playful circles around them. Pausing at the foot of the stairs, Dag apologized: "I'm sorry I was so sarcastic with Thorstein. He is your guest, too, and I should have curbed my tongue; but, by the Aesir, I find it hard to stomach ignorant arrogance!"

"Never you mind, Dag. You were more gentle with Thorstein than he deserved." The weather-beaten face broke into a grin. "But, oh, just imagine the expression on his face if he actually knew the truth of the matter. What a delicious joke. Sleep you well, my friend."

"Sleep you well, Agnar," Dag chuckled, his good

humor restored. Followed closely by Ledgi, Dag mounted
the stairs and entered the loft, while below Agnar paused
briefly to admire the beauty of the starry sky before
returning to the cozy warmth of his hall.

⌘

Dvalin's Doom

Deep within the endless labyrinth of grottoes and tunnels that run throughout the realm of Svartalfheim, an ominous hush had fallen. The anvils where a legion of dwarvish smiths hammered out the finest metalwork in the Nine Worlds, be it a rune sword or jewelled cloak-clasp, lay silent for the first time in memory. An aura of dread and expectation permeated the cool underworld air, for Motsognir the Mighty, ruler of the dwarves since the Nine Worlds began, lay dying—and neither of his sub-chiefs, Durin and Dvalin, had yet been proclaimed his heir. The dwarves had known no ruler save Motsognir, so most of them were both saddened at the prospect of losing one who had been like a father to his people and apprehensive about a future without him. The uncertainty about his successor only added to their concern, for neither Durin nor Dvalin was loved by all.

In the sleeping chamber of Motsognir, it was a solemn group that stood beside their dying leader's bed. His daughter, Runa, sat on the edge of the bed, holding his withered hand, his wife having long since preceded him into Hel's domain. Durin and Dvalin looked on in silence, shadows cast by the flickering candlelight high-lighting the lines of concern and frustration etched in their faces. Only Motsognir's councillors disturbed the silence with their guarded whispers.

"Surely he cannot live much longer. Why won't he name his successor?"

"He must, he must. If he does not, Durin and Dvalin will be at each other's throat before his body is cold."

"Hush, hush," an incredibly old voice wheezed. "I may be dying, but there's nothing wrong with my hear-ing. And I'm sure Durin and Dvalin can hear you, too." Motsognir's voice seemed to gain strength as he contin-ued to speak. "I have not waited this long to name my heir in order to cause them—or you—anxiety. I would not be so cruel. No, I have waited because the choice was not a clear one, and because it was so terribly important. Remember our saying: 'Earth ways are seldom hasty, but they are almost always certain.'"

"'Was important' your majesty said, not 'is important,'" gulped Thekk, the chief councillor. "Does that mean you have reached a decision?"

"Yes, I have, old friend." And everyone leaned forward in anticipation. "But before I reveal it, there are some things I want to say to all of you. Runa, my child, help me to sit up so I can breathe more easily." And as

66   Thekk gently raised the old chieftain into a sitting position, Motsognir's daughter propped up some more pillows against which he leaned back with a sigh.

"Thank you, my dear. And thank you, Thekk. Now, hear me out and you will, I hope, come to understand why I have chosen as I have. Indulge an old dwarf because of the love you bear for him . . . and because he is still your king!" Pride and authority rang in his voice, and his previously pallid features shone with the strength of yesteryear.

"You must remember that we dwarves are a mighty race with a proud heritage. Men do not call us the Dark Elves without reason, though they—and many of you younger dwarves—may have forgotten why. The story that the first dwarves were formed from maggots that crawled in the giant Ymir's corpse was a wicked lie, fomented by those who wish us ill—Loki's doing as likely as not. No, we came not from maggots, but from the same stock as the Light Elves." He paused for effect. "We—and they—are what we are by choice. Once there were just the elves, neither Dark nor Light, and then Njuollo Arrow-Swift saved Odin from the clutches of a ravenous ice-bear. In gratitude, the Father of the Gods offered the elves their choice of two worlds: Alfheim, a wide, sunlit land, which lay hard by the gods' own realm of Asgard and was subject to their rule; and a much vaster underground kingdom he proposed to call Svartalfheim because its inhabitants would be privileged to dwell for all time in the Land of Always Night. To those who chose Svartalfheim, Odin also gave the magical mastery of metalworking—a gift denied to those who chose to remain Above, exposed to the harsh glare of sunlight beneath a sky roof so high that none could hope to touch it." Motsognir shuddered momentarily at the thought of such unlimited open spaces. "As a final gift to those who chose independence and metalworking skill, the Allfather changed our forms so that we would be well suited for our new home—he shortened our stature so we could slip in and out of small tunnels, gave us owllike eyes so we could see well in dim light, enlarged our ears so we could catch the faintest sounds, and made our noses so keen we could detect the slightest odors. Was ever a people more blessed?" The old dwarf sighed contentedly.

"Still, those who chose to stay Above seem to be content with their lot, too, or so their traders would have us believe when we meet them Above at night from time to time to exchange our metalwork for their game and hides. It is hard to imagine how that could be so, but perhaps it is because they know no better."

Motsognir pondered this thought for a moment before continuing. "Yet it is good that they do not or they might covet what we possess and, kinfolk or not, Svartalfheim is for the dwarves—and the dwarves alone! Nobody, not even the gods, tells us what to do; and if someone wants something from us, why, he has to ask for it politely—cap in hand, so to speak—and pay the price we demand. That is how it has always been and that is the way it should always be!"

None would have known from Motsognir's ringing voice that the dwarf king was so near death as to be able to see the dim outline of Hel's Gate. But then this burst of energy passed and he seemed to slump forward.

"Which is why I have chosen Durin as my successor," Motsognir stated quietly. "He will preserve and perpetuate our honored traditions, and thus he will insure that the dwarves remain independent and prosperous. Dvalin is a fine dwarf, too—and none can ever forget that he is the one who secured the secret of the runes for dwarfkind—but I see him as too much the dreamer, too enchanted by change just for the sake of doing something different, to have the ultimate responsibility and authority for deciding the future of our race. Such attributes would make him a splendid advisor, but the kingship requires greater stability. I am sorry, Dvalin; I know you must be bitterly disappointed, but it was my decision to make. I can only hope you will give Durin as much support and loyalty as you have always given me." Motsognir cast a concerned glance at Dvalin, who stood stiffly with his fists clenched and his lips set in a grim line, then slowly scanned the faces of the rest of the assemblage before smiling into Runa's tear-filled eyes.

"I must be going now, friends, for Hel's Gate is swinging wide to receive me. Grieve not, Runa, for when I see your dear mother I shall give her your love." With a final sigh, Motsognir's shade slipped away from among them, leaving behind a maelstrom of seething emotions—grief and relief, triumph and rage.

~

"I won't have it! I tell you, Thekk, I just won't have it. Was I Motsognir's choice or wasn't I?" demanded Durin in a loud voice.

"Of course you were, your majesty," replied the chief councillor soothingly.

"Well, you would never know it the way Dvalin struts about, followed by his admirers. No, don't bother trying to deny it," Durin raised his hand as Thekk seemed about to speak. "Dvalin does have a large group of followers who were not pleased with Motsognir's choice. I suspect that even Runa would have preferred Dvalin, which is probably why she journeyed to Asgard to join the Sisterhood of Norns. That way she would not have to be disloyal to the memory of her father."

Thekk stared at his toes. "I'm afraid your majesty may be right." Then the chief councillor looked up. "But I hope your majesty knows he can count on my loyalty?"

"I have never doubted your loyalty to Motsognir or to his chosen successor, Thekk, though I must confess I am beginning to grow suspicious of nearly everyone else." Durin sighed discontentedly.

"Then your majesty is going to have to do something at once," responded Thekk. "Svartalfheim cannot have two rulers—in fact, or in appearance."

"Well, I'm certainly not to going to hand the crown over to Dvalin; you can be sure of that. If Motsognir had thought him to be the best choice, he would have named Dvalin king to begin with. No, that's no answer. And trying to reason with Dvalin to gain his cooperation has proven to be utterly useless so far." Durin threw up his hands in exasperation.

Slumping back in his throne, the dwarf king tented his fingers and pressed them against his chin. "Well, I suppose I would be within my rights to execute him for treason . . . ."

At that declaration, a loud gasp was heard and a pretty female dwarf emerged from the tapestries behind the throne. She flung herself at the feet of the amazed king and open-mouthed councillor as she gasped out, "Oh, my brother, surely you could not be so heartless! I know you are unhappy because Dvalin is so well liked, and he won't bow and scrape to you, but I can't believe

70   you would have him killed for that."

"Dear Brunni, if you've eavesdropped for more than just a moment you'll realize that you're judging me unfairly. Still," Durin paused with a puzzled expression on his face, "I don't understand why my own sister should be such a staunch supporter of Dvalin."

Brunni tossed her head of rich brown hair and proudly, almost defiantly, declared: "Because I love him."

Durin clapped his hands over his ears and groaned aloud. "That does it! Now he has even turned my own sister against me." He leaped up from his throne and glared at Brunni. "Listen to me, and listen well. For your sake—and because I don't relish making Dvalin a martyr—I will spare his life. But," said Durin, raising a silencing hand to cut off his sister's cry of relief and gratitude, "he cannot remain in Svartalfheim to continue undermining my authority. Thekk, draw up the proclamation of banishment at once."

As Brunni's eyes grew wide with horror, Durin continued, "While I would like nothing better than to have Dvalin discover on his own what life without Svartalfheim will be like, I don't wish to have his followers stirring up trouble after he is gone, so all who wish to follow him into exile may leave Svartalfheim forever. I insist only that they leave their women and children here until a safe new home has been built for them." Of course, thought Durin to himself, that could well take several years, time enough, perhaps, for Brunni to come to her senses and forget Dvalin.

~

Quaffing ale and swapping stories with "good old

Dvalin" was one thing; leaving wife and child for several years to venture into the unknown, far from familiar and beloved Svartalfheim, was quite another. In the end, fewer than two dozen dwarves chose to accompany Dvalin into exile.

Many a tear was shed and many a longing look was cast the evening that Dvalin's band took leave of their loved ones and departed from their mountain home. Brunni clung desperately to Dvalin until he gently freed himself from her embrace and assumed his position at the head of the column. He had promised to send for her once the new dwarf colony was established—its caverns hollowed and tunnels dug—but when you are young (for a dwarf) and in love, a separation of several years seems like forever and such a promise is hollow comfort, indeed. Thus it was that just a few nights later a shadowy figure, wearing a hooded cloak and carrying a backpack stuffed with food and other necessities, slipped unseen through an unguarded tunnel. Without casting so much as a single regretful backward glance, Brunni moved swiftly down the boulder-strewn slope toward Svarinshaug, the huge barrow mound that she knew the refugees planned to use as a way-station before continuing on their journey.

So intent was the dwarf-maid on reaching Svarinshaug and her lover's arms that she failed to pay attention to all of her senses, and thus did not detect the rank odor of troll until what appeared to be a huge boulder along the trail reached out a long, hairy arm and plucked Brunni off her feet.

"Well, well, well . . . and what have we here? Another of those pesky thumblings, I should think," rasped the troll's harsh voice. "Only this one hasn't gotten away from us like the others, has it? Oh, no, indeed it hasn't."

"Here, now, Ogmund," snarled another large "boulder" as it detached itself from the mountainside and reached out a grasping hand for Brunni, "let me have it, won't you? It was my big toe nearly got chopped off by one of them little axes when we tried to grab us a couple thumblings down by the barrow mound last night. I guess I owe them something for my toe, I do, so let me have this one." His hand fixed on Brunni's cloak and he pulled her toward him.

Ogmund glowered and tugged in the opposite direction. With a loud rip, the cloak tore in two and Brunni fell to the ground with a thump. Unfortunately for the dwarf-maid, the fall stunned her long enough for Ogmund to grab her again before she could scramble away.

"See here, Kor," declared Ogmund, "if we fight over her, she might get away. Let's decide together what to do with her."

"That's a good idea, Ogmund," agreed his companion, "my sore toe was just making me greedy for revenge. What shall we do, tear her in half and eat her?"

"No-o-o," drawled Ogmund. "We just split that deer between us and I'm not the least bit hungry. Let's do something different, something that will teach the other thumblings a lesson."

"Sounds good to me," responded Kor enthusiastically, "you got an idea?"

"You know what happens to trolls who are struck by sunlight, don't you?" queried Ogmund.

"Sure do," Kor shuddered. "They turn to stone."

"Well," grinned Ogmund, "I've heard that the same thing happens to thumblings, on account of their living underground like us. Why don't we tie this one down somewhere and find out what sunlight does to her? If we put her down by the river just before dawn, won't that be a nasty little surprise for the others to find when they go there to get water tomorrow night?"

"It will be if it works," muttered Kor. "What if nothing happens to her when the sun comes up?"

"Can you imagine the wolves or the eagles letting a tasty little morsel like this stay uneaten all day? Oh, no, friend Kor, her doom is sealed any way you look at it." And Ogmund chuckled gleefully, very much pleased with himself.

~

Shortly before dawn, Dvalin had been wandering—bow in hand—in search of game in the alder thickets near the river when his keen ears detected what sounded like pitiful sobbing. Suspecting that it might be a ruse by those pesky trolls his band had barely escaped the other night, Dvalin approached the source of the sobs with all his senses alert. He was also mindful that dawn was rapidly approaching and that it must not find him very far from the barrow mound. His hooded cloak would give him some protection, but he knew he dare not turn his face toward the naked sun. Although the sun's rays would not turn dwarves to stone—as it would trolls—it assuredly would render a dwarf permanently blind, another facet of Father Odin's "gift." When the ancestral Dark Elves had agreed to forego the light of the sun, they had, indeed, relinquished it forever.

At the edge of the alder thicket, Dvalin paused. Extending thence to the river's edge was a broad meadow.

74   In the center of the meadow, a tall sapling had been stripped of its limbs and driven as deep into the turf as a powerful pair of troll arms could manage. At the base of the crude pole, a writhing white object appeared to be the source of the sobs. Even though the sky was becoming lighter, Dvalin's curiosity drew him ever closer until, to his horror, he recognized a naked Brunni bound hand and foot to the pole in such a way that she faced eastward. A quick glance at the horizon confirmed her imminent peril from the rising sun, and Dvalin dashed across the remaining space to cut her loose and try to find some shelter in the alder thicket for both of them before it was too late.

"Oh, Dvalin, you've come, you've come," Brunni cried.

"No time to talk now," Dvalin grunted as he sawed at the heavy bindings the trolls had used. "I've got to get you out of here before the sun comes up."

One by one the cords parted, and it seemed as if victory were almost in their grasp. Then—just as the last cord fell away and Brunni was free to stumble along on her numb, chafed legs—the hunting cry of a king eagle, largest and most ferocious of the birds of prey, shattered the eastern sky and froze the hearts of the two dwarves with terror. Dvalin realized at once that they could never reach the cover of the alders before the king eagle seized one of them, yet if they stayed to fight, the rising sun would blind them.

In almost a single motion, Dvalin whipped the hooded cloak from his shoulders and pulled it over Brunni. Forcing her to the ground with her now hooded head turned away from the sun—and admonishing her not to move for any reason—Dvalin nocked an arrow to his bowstring. Hearing the triumphant scream of the king eagle as it started to dive toward its prey, and knowing that the bird would attack with the sun at its back, Dvalin turned to face his enemy—to gain one glimpse of it with his last sight. There it was . . . and coming incredibly fast! Yet the afterimage of that one last vision was burned on his brain, and when he drew back his bowstring and loosed his arrow it was as if he saw the bird still. With the arrow, Dvalin also loosed a fearful cry, "Odin-n-n-n!" But whether that cry was meant as a prayer of supplication or as a curse, none ever knew save Dvalin.

The shot was true and, although the tumbling body of the king eagle struck Dvalin and knocked him asprawling over Brunni, the bird was dead before it ever touched the ground.

Dvalin gained much honor that day—as well as the nickname Solblindi, which he was to carry the rest of his life. When night fell, he and Brunni returned to the barrow mound where they were married at once, dwarf-style. His band remained in Svarinshaug for only a short while before moving on to the brooding mountain called Aurvanger, which sits by itself in the middle of Joru Plain. In time, after Dvalin's followers revisited Svartalfheim to reclaim their families and bring them back to Aurvanger, the tale of Brunni's rescue and Dvalin's sacrifice became common knowledge—and from that time on the sun was known among dwarvish folk as "Dvalin's Doom."

⌘

The Blood-Red Rune

The western coast of Midgard was dotted with thousands of islands, ranging from tiny, rocky skerries on which no vegetation grew, to some quite large enough to support forests and villages. The one that lay farthest from the mainland, Ytre Öy—the Outermost Isle, was of middling size and, though grassy, generally lacked trees. 'Twas here that the mighty wizard Vilmeid came to study his magic arts in solitude, far from the prying eyes of neighbors.

Still the sea can be crossed, and late one evening the dwarf Runa presented herself at Vilmeid's sod-roofed, timbered hall, and announced she had come with the prophecy that he had requested from the Norns. Surprisingly, Vilmeid reacted to her declaration with anything but pleasure. The richly robed, grey-bearded wizard folded his arms and glowered down in disbelief at the diminutive messenger who boldly stood before him, her hooded head barely topping his knee.

"Do the Norns think to insult me?" he snapped, his

eyebrows furrowing ominously. "I knew that the Three would have to remain at Urd's Well, but to send a lowly dwarf to me with their prophecy?" His nose wrinkled with disdain. "Vilmeid is no mere bush wizard, woman, to settle for scraps from a jarl's table. I can make—or unmake—such men with a snap of my fingers, and those great lords are all careful not to annoy me . . . very careful, indeed. The Norns, too, would be wise not to arouse my enmity."

"And you would be wise, Vilmeid, not to see insult where none was intended," retorted Runa, pushing back the hood to reveal her owl-like eyes and large, pointed ears. "Save for the Three, none of the Sisterhood enjoys higher status than another, be she dwarf, or elf, or Aesir-kin. And," her voice bristled as she planted her hands on her hips, "you can be sure that I would not have come to Ytre Öy save in dire need. No dwarf likes the sea, and I'm still queasy from the boat trip over here. But none of the other Sisters was available just now, so the Three sent me—and whether I like it, or you like it, is of no consequence."

"Don't be cheeky with me if you value your life," Vilmeid snarled as, bending down, he shook his forefinger under Runa's nose. The dwarf disdained a reply and the two just stood, glaring at each other, for a long minute. Then the wizard "humphed" and, turning, mounted the dais where he seated himself in his throne-like chair, ornately carved with figures of dragons.

"Well, get on with it," he said, grumpily. "If you've brought a prophecy, let me hear it . . . and then begone. But," and he shook his finger again admonishingly, "you can be sure that the Three are going to hear from me, too."

The dwarf stood facing Vilmeid, her hands clasped at her waist, and recited in a singsong manner. "I, Runa, bring Vilmeid these words of Skuld, who has looked at the strands of his life's web and seen his fate:

> *'Vilmeid's own art shall be his bane,*
> *His precious life-force out shall drain.*
> *This wizard's end shall he meet soon,*
> *When he beholds the blood-red rune.' "*

"Whaaat?" Vilmeid shrilled incredulously and leapt to his feet. "You have the audacity to stand there and tell me that I should fear a rune, I who am the greatest runemaster in the Nine Worlds? Skuld must have taken complete leave of her senses to make such a ridiculous prophecy."

"Skuld never makes a mistake," insisted Runa stubbornly. "She said that a blood-red rune would mark your doom, and that is what she meant."

"Would you dare question my mastery of the runes, you miserable worm?" Vilmeid raged, thoroughly incensed at what he perceived as Runa's insolent obstinance. "Then you shall become one. The ancient tales say that the first dwarves were created from the maggots that fed on the giant Ymir's corpse. It seems only fitting that you should end as your race began—crawling, blind and mindless, in the bowels of the earth."

A cruel smile played across the wizard's thin lips as he stepped forward and extended his arms above the now thoroughly frightened, but still defiant, dwarf. Drawing upon the enormous cosmic power he had learned to tap, Vilmeid sketched a series of icy blue runes in the air. They seemed to waver and flow together, then settled on Runa's forehead. She screamed only once before her features, too, flowed into shapelessness, and she shrank into the worm form her tormentor had decreed. Vilmeid disdainfully scooped her up in an old slipper and deposited her outside in the herb garden, muttering that now she might finally make herself useful.

Vilmeid did not sleep particularly well that night; not because of any remorse about his treatment of Runa, but because Skuld's message haunted him. Could there be some aspect of the runic arts that he had failed to master? No, of that he was certain. Perhaps some obscure bit of arcane knowledge he had overlooked? Not likely . . . yet not impossible. Vilmeid wrestled with the problem until dawn when, after a quick and barely noticed breakfast, he concluded that the best defense against an attack of whatever kind—by weapons or by magic—would be to set up a protective runestone at each of the four cardinal points of the island, and to imbue them with a goodly part of his own power.

After all, safe behind the rune ward thus created, he would not need nearly so much personal power. The decision made, he at once set about preparing the stones, and by day's end the rune ward was in place. Exhausted both by his efforts and the partial loss of his power, Vilmeid collapsed in his bed, satisfied that the barrier would be proof against any assault. Let the Norns, or anyone else, do their worst!

$\sim$

As he came in sight of the large spring called Urd's Well, which lay close beside a great root of the World Tree—Yggdrasil—Thor Redbeard's legs still tingled slightly from having waded through the four icy streams that rushed across his path. He was a bit puzzled when he failed to see any of the Norns, the wisewomen who use the water of the Well—mixed with the white clay that encircles it—to heal the Tree, assailed as it is, root and bough, by destructive cosmic forces. For in fact, the Norns' daily task of applying the healing white paste to the trunk of Yggdrasil is even more important than their role as the caretakers of the Loom of Life and interpreters of the Tapestry of Wyrd. Should Yggdrasil die, the Nine Worlds would disintegrate and all existence cease!

Drawing near to the Well, Thor was startled to hear the sound of weeping coming from the hall of the Norns. He could not recall ever before having seen or heard one of the Sisterhood cry, though their knowledge of the past, present, and future of all beings in the Nine Worlds might well have given them cause to weep long before now. Thor shuddered to think what frightful event must have befallen—or soon would—and he broke into a run toward the door of the hall.

Pausing at the portal only long enough to announce his presence by thumping his huge fist on the wooden door frame, which was entwined with carved, leafy representations of the Tree, Thor strode into the hall. No lesser Norns were to be seen, but the Three—ancient Urd, matronly Verdandi, and youthful Skuld —huddled close together, obviously shaken with grief.

"Why, whatever is the matter," inquired Thor, "to upset you so? Is Ragnarök upon us?"

"No, Thor," sobbed white-haired Urd, the tears running in rivulets down her wrinkled face. "It's the wizard Vilmeid . . . ."

"He's destroyed one of our Sisters," wept beautiful Verdandi, who always reminded Thor of his own beloved wife, Sif.

"Dear little Runa," wailed Skuld, her eyes swollen and the creamy complexion of her seeming girlhood soured with red splotches and stained with tears.

Eventually they managed to pour out the whole horrible tale, with Thor first shocked and then increasingly angry. His eyes took on the fiery glint that many a giant or troll had seen—much to their regret.

"What do you plan to do to him?" Thor asked them in a barely controlled voice. "Whatever it is, he deserves something worse."

"We can do nothing, Redbeard; it is not our way," replied Urd. "While it is true that we look after the Tapestry of Wyrd, we are actually the observers and foretellers of fate—not its manipulators. We neither create nor control it, whatever gods or men may think." She pointed a bony forefinger at him. "I remember that which has been."

Verdandi added: "I see that which is."

Skuld concluded: "And I foresee that which shall be. The past that Urd remembers and the present that Verdandi sees help create the future that I foresee. Vilmeid will not escape his fate, for he has shaped its weaving."

"I'm confused," muttered Thor. "You say you Norns don't control fate, but then you tell me that miserable wizard cannot escape his fate. Deep thinking may not be my strong point, but even I can see the contradiction there."

Urd's ancient face crinkled with gentle amusement. "It isn't so much a matter that he cannot escape as that he *will* not. Let me explain. You see, Thor, all beings begin life limited by the very nature of what they are—Aesir and humans obviously have very different limitations. Within those limitations, however, each individual's portion of the Tapestry is affected by all sorts of things—by kinfolk and friends, by enemies, and by the situations one encounters during a lifetime. The ways one chooses to respond to each of these make up the horizontal strands of the weft on our loom." While she paused, Skuld and Verdandi nodded their agreement. "At the beginning of a being's life there is no single fate ordained; there are only numerous possibilities—the vertical strands of the loom's warp. But each weft strand chosen narrows the possibilities and, at the same time, establishes patterns of choice-making . . . and so the weaving wends its way. For most beings, once their patterns are firmly established, future choices become very limited and their fate's design is pretty well determined."

Skuld interjected in her sweet, almost childlike voice, "That's what we really do; we read patterns. And even if someone tries to escape his fate, he usually follows the patterns he's been weaving throughout his life. That's why my prophecies are almost never wrong."

Verdandi rose and placed her hands on the back of Skuld's shoulders. "Still, it is not impossible for someone with sufficient wisdom—and humility—to deliberately choose to alter his behavior. However, you needn't fear that Vilmeid will avoid his fate." Her upper lip curled scornfully. "It's not in his nature to change his own patterns—he has too high an opinion of himself for that."

"This is all very interesting, but I'm more given to action than philosophy," growled Thor, pounding his fist in the palm of his other hand. "Is there anything in the laws that says I can't try to hasten him along his fated road to Hel's gate?"

"Go with our blessings," said Urd, rising shakily to her feet and leaning on her intricately carved walking stick. And Thor rushed off to his own hall, many-roomed Bilskirnir, to fetch his goat cart and his terrible hammer, Mjöllnir.

~

The following morning a shame-faced Thor tentatively entered the hall of the Norns.

"I hate to admit it," he exclaimed huskily, "but I have failed you—and poor little Runa. Vilmeid has warded Ytre Öy with such powerful runes that I couldn't get close to it. Finally, in desperation, I hurled Mjöllnir at his hall, hoping to blast the roof off and flush the old fox from his lair, but the hammer seemed to hit some invisible barrier above the island and bounced away." Thor whistled ruefully. "I had no idea there were any wizards who could command such power!"

"He is the greatest of them all—in terms of runelore," said Verdandi, "but the least in terms of compassion and humility."

"But you musn't trouble yourself on that account, young Thor." Urd gave him a soft, but somehow almost sinister, smile. "Skuld has something to say to you."

"I know that we are pledged not to interfere," Skuld said, looking at her feet. Then she raised her deep blue eyes to stare full into Thor's, "but we Three have agreed that I can tell you something of what I saw in the Tapestry this morning. It was rain, Thor, torrents of rain . . . falling on Ytre Öy. More than that I cannot say, for even Norns can bend the laws just so far." She looked at him appealingly. "Do you understand what I am saying?"

Puzzled, Thor looked deep into her eyes for several moments, then comprehension smoothed his furrowed brow. "Yes, I believe I do. I'm not at all sure I see how it will help, but I think I know what you want me to do—and I'll do it." With a reassuring smile, Thor once more took his leave.

The Three-who-are-One looked at each other with satisfaction, and the hall by Urd's Well rang with their triumphant laughter.

~

Driving his goat cart through the sky, Thor herded the storm clouds from far and near to form an ever-growing, ever-darkening mass over Ytre Öy. When it seemed the clouds could tower no higher nor the sky grow darker, he galloped into the heart of the mass, hurling thunderbolts left and right in wild abandon—truly the storm god in his element. Thus assaulted, the clouds relinquished their watery burden, and the rain began to pelt the island—first in increasingly large drops, but then in sheets. Whenever the storm gave signs of letting up, Thor would round up new clouds to renew the attack. And so it continued for nine days.

Snug in his hall, Vilmeid had been somewhat annoyed at the inconvenience of being trapped indoors, but he was unconcerned about the ultimate outcome. The Outermost Isle was high and generally well drained, so there was no possibility of it being flooded, if that was Thor's intention. Had there been such a danger, Vilmeid would have directed the rune ward to deflect rain as well. No, Redbeard was probably just venting his frustration in this childish fashion.

On the evening of the ninth day the rain ceased and the tattered remnants of the storm clouds scudded off to the east, pursued by a stiff sea breeze. Vilmeid emerged from his hall to enjoy the fresh air and watch the setting sun from Ytre Öy's western headland. The walk to the headland was slowed by the soggy condition of the ground, so the sun wheel was already passing over the horizon, casting a golden path to the island by the time Vilmeid reached the slight embankment just above the runestone he had raised there.

The stone appeared to be slightly tilted, perhaps having settled unevenly in the soggy soil, so Vilmeid started down the embankment to reset it properly. He stepped on something small and wiggly, a worm driven out by the rain. Without pausing, he deliberately crushed it underfoot but, in doing so, lost his footing on the slick and slimy surface. The wizard's feet shot out from under him and he tumbled head-over-heels down the slope, coming to a halt only when his head hit the corner of the runestone with a loud and sickening crack. The force of the impact split his skull and toppled the runestone.

Vilmeid lay sprawled against the fallen stone, like a broken doll discarded by a thoughtless child, and felt his life ebbing away. With so much of his power invested in the now useless rune ward, the wizard was helpless to heal himself. He drifted in and out of consciousness for a time before descending into the final darkness. His vision dimming, the last sight Vilmeid beheld was his own blood staining one of the runes red, the ᚲ-rune—the rune of fate!

⌘

The Kraken Cup

Storrad the Proud was a viking fierce, and a wizard of no little skill. This deadly combination permitted Storrad and his followers to terrorize the western coast of Midgard. In their shallow-bottomed dragon ships they would swoop down on unsuspecting coastal villages, carry off everything worth taking, and—as they departed—put the village to the torch.

Carried away by their easy successes, and rather frustrated by how little gold and silver they had seized, Storrad set his sights on bigger prey—Hlesöy, the legendary island stronghold of the giant Aegir, who with his mermaid wife, Ran, ruled the sea and gathered the treasures from all the ships that sank beneath the waves. In this task they were assisted by their nine daughters and

the other merfolk. Most sea raiders gave Hlesöy a very
wide berth, wisely choosing not to challenge Aegir and
the merfolk, but Storrad had great faith in his abilities as
a wizard and strategist— and an even greater hunger for
the treasures of Hlesöy.

Thus it was that one morning Storrad's three
dragon ships came sailing toward a strange fog bank that
rested upon the sea off the coast of Alfheim. As the ships
breasted the rolling swells, the men soon noticed the
heads of giant women breaking the surface of the water,
their long green hair floating out beside them. Curiosity
about the strangers who had invaded their part of the sea
had drawn Aegir's daughters to the ships.

This curiosity was just what Storrad had been
counting on, and had alerted his men to expect. So the
warriors kept their weapons out of sight, smiled and
called to the mermaids, and waved bright necklaces and
other jewelry that might warm a woman's heart.

Delighted by their visitors' friendliness and
apparent offer of gifts, the mermaids threw caution to the
winds, swam right up to the ships, and grasped the gunwales with one hand while reaching for the trinkets with
the other. Alas for them, the ships' hulls had been
magicked by Storrad, and the mermaids were trapped—
stuck fast to the gunwales!

Storrad's little fleet and its captives were able to sail
right up to Hlesöy and anchor in the shallows along its
rocky shore, for the fog bank had lifted the moment the
mermaids were captured. Leaving some warriors to guard
the ships and the captives still attached to them, Storrad
led the rest of his viking band into Aegir's rocky hall.

Storrad's eyes grew round and his greedy heart beat
faster at the sight of that hall, whose walls were covered

with so much gleaming gold that it needed no other source of illumination.

Aegir and Ran had known of the raiders' coming, for word travels swiftly in the sea, but—fearing for their daughters' safety—there seemed to be nothing they could do to defend themselves or their realm. Aegir remained seated on his throne while Ran reclined in a nearby pool of water connected to the sea. She had tried to swim out to comfort her daughters, but Storrad had magically sealed off the watergate so Ran was forced to bide her time. Storrad, it seemed, firmly held the upper hand.

While Storrad shouted directions—and Aegir and Ran glumly watched—the raiders scurried about gathering up all the gold, silver, and jewelry they could find. And there was much, for the sea takes its toll. The men were just beginning to rip the gold plating down from the walls when Storrad's eyes fell upon a strange-looking drinking cup sitting in a wall recess beside Aegir's throne. The large cup seemed to be fashioned from a single piece of jadelike stone that glowed with a soft green light. The handle was shaped like a squid's tentacle and wrapped about the body of the cup. Storrad picked up the cup and examined it curiously.

"Well, what do we have here?" he mused thoughtfully.

Aegir spoke for the first time. "It's called the Kraken Cup, and I'd leave it here if I were you. It's much too dangerous to be kept anywhere other than Hlesöy."

"Oh, really?" said Storrad, now thoroughly intrigued. "Why don't you just tell me about it. We have all the time in the world."

"As you wish," replied Aegir.

~

A great Kraken, a squid as large as a small island, **89** had taken up residence off the coast not many leagues from Hlesöy. Traveling beneath the waves it would swallow whole schools of fish in a single gulp. But that was not enough to quell its enormous appetite, so often the Kraken would float at the surface, its smooth, leathery back resembling nothing so much as a huge treeless skerry. Then, when some unwary air breather approached—be it a seal, a whale, or a fisherman—the Kraken would plunge powerfully backward toward the bottom of the sea, its sudden departure from the surface creating a huge whirlpool that sucked its prey downward, too, until the great tentacles wrapped around the victim and stuffed it into the Kraken's mouth.

Now "kill to live" is a rule of the sea, so I could hardly blame the Kraken for trying to survive. Still its presence in these waters was a threat to the lives and livelihood of my merfolk and our sea-elf friends, so I sent word by seagull to my grandson Heimdall—who, as you may have heard, knows a thing or two about magic, and is a handy fellow to have around when trouble comes calling.

Well, as soon as the gull had delivered its message, Heimdall galloped across the Rainbow Bridge and didn't stop riding until he had reached Riddo, the sea-elf village on the coast opposite Hlesöy. Leaving his faithful steed, Gulltopp, in the care of the elves, Heimdall went down to the water's edge, unrolled a seal skin he'd carried behind his saddle, and changed himself into a seal. Yes, I did say a seal. You needn't look so surprised—his nine mothers being mermaids, he can do that, you know.

At any rate, Heimdall swam over to Hlesöy as fast as his flippers would carry him, not stopping until he had popped up out of that pool over there and shed his seal skin. I led him right up to the top of Hlesöy's highest hill and pointed in the direction where the Kraken had last been seen. Large as the beast was, it was much too distant for me to see, but far-sighted Heimdall spotted it at once. I could tell by the look on his face and the way he let out his breath that he was terribly unhappy about what he was looking at.

"I had no idea that the creature was so large, grandfather. I can see why you want to get rid of it—he'll eat you out of house and home in no time." Heimdall cupped his chin in one hand and was silent for a time. "I can't imagine how I could attack the Kraken from the outside, but if I could just get him to swallow something . . . ."

"How do you expect to do that, my boy, and live to tell the story? Even if you could carry something close to him in your seal form, you could never hope to swim away fast enough to escape from his whirlpool and tentacles."

"True enough, grandfather, but if one of your orc-whale friends would agree to help, I just might be able to do it."

Well, that's just the way it turned out. Whales are really quite intelligent, you know, and all too many of them had fallen victim to the Kraken's bottomless appetite, so I had no trouble persuading one of the great orc-whales to accompany Heimdall when he paddled off in a little sealhide coracle to approach the Kraken. Heimdall and the whale didn't speak aloud as you and I do, but they talked mind to mind in pictures.

Anyway, when they had come as close to the squid's head as they dared, Heimdall unwrapped a large green stone he'd been carrying in his tunic, wedged it firmly in the framework of the coracle, and chanted a series of powerful runes over it. Immediately the stone began to glow and throb and give off the strongest odor of ripe fish you've ever smelled. That odor really caught the Kraken's attention and he began his backward dive.

Heimdall leapt into the water and grabbed the orc-whale's dorsal fin; then the two of them left the area as fast as that whale could swim. They were caught by the far edge of the whirlpool and it was touch-and-go for a moment or two, but orc-whales are powerful swimmers and they managed to escape the pull of the diving Kraken.

What happened to the Kraken? Well, the coracle with the green stone was swept round and round the whirlpool until his tentacles embraced the little boat and stuffed it into his mouth. Then the strangest thing happened. Once the Kraken swallowed that green stone, he couldn't stop swallowing! From the tip of the tentacle he had used to stuff the coracle into his mouth right on back to his diving fins, he swallowed himself up. The sea rushed in to fill up all that space, and just for a short time there was a far larger whirlpool than any the Kraken had created during his lifetime. Then all was calm, as if the Kraken had never existed.

A few days later one of my merfolk popped out of the pool carrying this cup, which he had found on the sea bottom where the Kraken had disappeared. Heimdall examined the cup carefully, declared it to be a fusion of the Kraken with the green stone he had swallowed, and said I should keep it as a remembrance. He also warned that in some strange way the Kraken lives on embodied in the cup, so that no one should ever drink from it—and no one ever has.

~

"No one ever has, eh? Well I guess I'll just have to be the first," declared Storrad boldly. "Have one of your servants fetch that mead for which your hall is so famous."

Aegir sighed, "I really wouldn't do that if I were you. Still, if you insist . . . ."

"I do insist," snapped Storrad impatiently.

Aegir signalled to one of his servants, and soon the man returned with a keg of mead and poured some of its golden contents into the Kraken Cup. After muttering a runic charm to offset any poison that might have been present in the cup or added to the mead, Storrad raised the cup to his lips. But, to his horror, no sooner had his lips touched the rim than the cup seemed to grow larger and take on a life of its own. The tentacle tip writhed free from the cup and wrapped itself around Storrad's neck. He had time to utter only one gurgling scream before he was pulled headfirst into the mouth of the cup and swallowed.

As Storrad's boots disappeared from sight, and the Kraken Cup shrank back to its normal size, Aegir mildly remarked: "Tsk, tsk, tsk. I did try to warn him."

Then the sea lord's expression hardened. "As for the rest of you, I think you'll find that your leader's magic perished with him and my daughters are no longer your hostages. So you had best begone—at once."

The leaderless vikings remained where they were standing in a dazed, horrified silence. Aegir rose to his full fifteen-foot height, pointed to the entrance way, and bellowed: "I said, BEGONE!"

That outburst broke the spell, and the vikings fell over each other in their rush to vacate the hall and get to their ships. Aegir followed them to the shore where the vikings were desperately trying to maneuver their dragon ships around for departure. The prevailing winds offered little help, so Aegir took out a triple-knotted wind cord a sea-elf wizard had given him and untied the first knot. Immediately a brisk wind began to blow seaward, and the dragon ships set sail.

The vikings were beginning to congratulate themselves on their good luck when Aegir loosened the second knot. The wind began to blow much harder, hurling the ships westward across the surface of the sea. Then, just when the ships appeared as little more than silhouettes against the horizon, Aegir undid the final knot and they were struck by a fierce tempest with gale-force winds, towering waves, and sea spouts. When the storm died down, there were no ships to be seen.

Aegir waded into the sea to embrace Ran and their daughters. "If any of the vikings lived through that storm," he mused, "sooner or later they'll be washed ashore on one of those little islands out there. When they find they have to survive on whatever fish they can catch, and comb the strand for driftwood to burn, then—perhaps—they will learn to value the real treasures of the sea."

⌘

The Gift

The power of *wyrd* works in mysterious ways, indeed. Had Aratak the Invincible, his silvery scales aglitter, not been driven by the mating urge to construct a glorious metallic bower for his lady love in the hopes of arousing her amorous instincts, it is unlikely that he and Prince Solvenn ever would have crossed paths. But *wyrd* will have its way . . . .

Solvenn's father, Ketil, king of Ormerdal, had died a short time back, and—having sent his spirit off to Valhalla with all due ceremony—the citizenry of Ormerdal were now gathered in Ormsby, the capital city, eagerly awaiting the coronation of their new king. Though the jarls occupied the places of honor as the ceremony got under way, all of the free farmers and tradesmen were there, too. Even the thralls had been given the day off in honor of the occasion, and they hung about on the outskirts gawking at the spectacle.

"Here comes the good part, Drott," remarked Kreggi, whose wits were sharper and knowledge of his betters more extensive than his fellow thrall's. "This is where the new king gets his hand cut and is blood-bound to the sword."

"Why would'ee wanta go and do that?" queried Drott. "A man gets cut often enough by chance . . . seems foolish to do it on purpose."

"You're the only fool around here, Drott," retorted Kreggi. "It's a magic sword, and there's some kind of spell on it. So long as the king has the sword, we'll have good harvests each year and lots of calves, lambs, and piglets."

"Humph," muttered Drott, "sounds like more work for the likes of you and me."

"More to eat for all of us, you should say. Now, hush, the prince has just bound himself to the sword. As soon as he sheaths it in the scabbard Princess Yrsa is holding, the ritual will be complete and he'll be declared king of Ormerdal." Kreggi heaved a sigh of satisfaction, both at the imminent completion of the event and his understanding of what it signified.

Kreggi's sigh came a moment too soon, however, for it was at just that instant the dragon Aratak—sailing high over Ormerdal—spotted the gleaming blade and decided it would be the ideal thing to top off the magnificent bower he had so painstakingly constructed. Visions of himself and the lovely Valdai the Strong-Willed rubbing neck scales, then writhing in reptilian bliss, flashed through his mind as he folded his leathery wings and hurled earthward. So preoccupied was he with his erotic fantasies that Aratak almost forgot to pull out of his dive in time.

Prince Solvenn had just raised the blade and was brandishing it above his head before stepping over to his wife to sheath it, when Aratak struck and wrenched the sword from the prince's grasp. Solvenn was knocked down by the force of the blow, while the dragon—trumpeting triumphantly—rose high into the sky and sailed southward toward the object of his affection. Pandemonium ensued . . . and reigned for quite some time thereafter.

~

"What's wrong with him, Bergljot?" demanded a distraught Yrsa of the small gray-haired woman who faced her. "You're a healer . . .you should know. His arm is nearly healed, but he is so weak and listless. He just sits around staring into space—half the time I don't think he knows I am in the same room with him!"

Bergljot frowned. "It is a sickness of the soul that ails the prince . . . and I fear its cause does not affect him alone. Many of the animals of Ormerdal have had stillbirths during these past weeks, and the crops are withering in the fields. The blessings bestowed by that sword in the past have become a curse now that the blade has been taken from us. Unless it is recovered, there can be little hope for either your husband or our poor land—both will fade and die."

Appalled, Yrsa stared open-mouthed at Bergljot, then gasped. "But Solvenn is in no condition to seek the sword. Why haven't any of the warriors gone? What are they waiting for?" Her voice rose shrilly. "And why wasn't I told all this before now?"

Bergljot laid a restraining hand on Yrsa's arm,

reflecting their long friendship. "Calm yourself, Princess. You were so concerned about your husband that no one wished to add to your burdens just yet." The healer paused, then continued. "As for why the warriors haven't gone after the sword . . . well, they are brave enough fighters, I suppose, but none of them has the stomach to meet a dragon face to face. And I can't say that I really blame them—no man is said to have overcome one of the greater orms since Vikar Wooden-Legs slew old Girkad Gleaming-Eye during the reign of King Alrek."

"Why did they call Vikar, Wooden-Legs?" asked Yrsa, calmer now and fascinated in spite of herself.

"Because the dragon's venom shriveled up his real legs and they had to be cut off afterwards," replied Bergljot matter-of-factly.

Yrsa made no effort to repress a shudder, but then stated resolutely, "Well, I just can't sit around here and watch my husband shrivel up and die—and Solvenn and I do have a responsibility for the well-being of this kingdom, too—so, if no one else is going to bring back that accursed sword, I suppose I will have to go."

Bergljot smiled slightly. "You are made of stronger stuff than I had thought, Princess, but who will you get to accompany you on a journey that ends in a dragon's lair? I would offer, if my gifts as a healer were not so badly needed here."

"I could not part from Solvenn with a clear conscience if I did not know you would be here to look after him, dear Bergljot," Yrsa reassured the older woman. "As for the others, I will not compel anyone to do out of duty what love and loyalty had not already inspired. No, it is better that I go alone. And fear not too much for my safety—I am not so fragile a blossom as some might think." A warm grin spread across her pretty round face. "Remember, I grew up playing rough and tumble with my three brothers."

"Would that Yngve, Yngvar, and Ygg were here when you need them, instead of gone off a-viking," muttered Bergljot.

"Well, they are not here and I am, so I'll just have to make the best of it. But, oh, Bergi, where should I go? How do I find one silvery dragon in a place as big as all Midgard? And if I don't find it quickly, by the time I do it won't really matter, will it?"

"You are right about that, Yrsa, but take heart for I think I can offer some good advice. Two days' ride to the south, on the western slopes of Rundhovd, is a small tarn. There lives the wisewoman Eren, one of the lesser norns. Like any of the Sisterhood, she knows much of what goes on in the Nine Worlds. The whereabouts of one particular dragon should pose no great problem for her."

Yrsa clasped Bergljot to her, hugging the healer warmly. "You are a true friend, Bergi. I begin to take hope. Give me your blessing, and I'll leave as soon as I can pack the things I need. Let no one know where I've gone until it is too late for anyone to stop me."

Bergljot nodded. "I will tell them you are feeling unwell and have taken to your bed closet, but that they need not worry because I am looking after you." The healer held Yrsa at arm's length and looked deep into her sky-blue eyes. "Go, Princess, and may the Lady Freyja—who is no 'fragile blossom' either—be with you on your quest. She always looks with favor on the plight of lovers."

Despite the urgency of Yrsa's mission—or, more likely, because of it—the ride to Rundhovd seemed to her to be painfully slow. The western slopes of the great mountain comprised a series of increasingly higher ridges, and the rough trail that ascended them wound ever upward, one switchback after another. The trail was narrow, with many steep dropoffs, so Yrsa wisely curbed her impatience and allowed her horse to set its own pace.

The farmer who had so graciously hosted Yrsa the previous evening when she had stopped for the night, had seen her off on the right trail this morning with good advice and good wishes . . . yet, as she rode away, he had shaken his head dubiously about the wisdom of a woman riding alone in such a place.

But none had barred her path—neither beast nor brigand—and as the chariot of the sun neared the western horizon, the trail topped a rise and Yrsa saw before her, nestled between two ridges, the tarn she had been seeking. Rush-bordered, its still, black waters mirroring the rays of the sinking sun, the tarn was a sight of such beauty and tranquility that Yrsa gave an involuntary gasp of delight and reined in her mount, the urgency of her quest giving way momentarily as a sense of peace came over her. After a minute or two, the young woman sighed and urged her horse on down the trail to the tarn.

As Yrsa drew near the tiny lake, she spied a small skin tent tucked into the birch woods that fringed the tarn. A wispy curl of smoke arising near the tent told Yrsa that Eren was at home, and it suddenly reminded the girl that she had had little to eat since breakfast. Yrsa gave a loud halloo, as courtesy and prudence required, before riding into the clearing that lay between the tent and the tarn.

Reining up, Yrsa looked curiously about her, wondering where the norn could be. A bubbling pot hung over the small fire, but Eren was nowhere to be seen. Yrsa was about to call out a second time, when a figure with a drawn bow and nocked arrow stepped out from the woods behind the tent. It appeared to be a woman, though rather than wearing the usual gray robes of a norn she was clad in close-fitting deerskin trousers and a baggy blue tunic girdled with a broad leather belt. Short leather boots were fastened to her feet by narrow wrappings that wound around her legs to midcalf. She was short in stature, but slender of frame, and her broad face bore a pointed chin and a long, narrow-bridged nose. Yrsa did not need to see the tips of the woman's slightly pointed ears, hidden beneath her short, curly brown hair, to realize that she was face to face with an elf.

Yrsa stammered, "I wa-was looking for Eren, the norn."

"Well, you found her," Eren replied as she replaced the arrow in her birchbark belt quiver and stood her bow against the tent wall. "Now will you please dismount and give your poor horse a rest, and a rubdown."

Yrsa complied with Eren's requests and, when the horse had been cared for, joined the elf-woman on a log by the fire for supper. Yrsa tried to explain her problem through a mouthful of boiled deer meat, but Eren silenced her with a raised forefinger. "Not now—we'll talk later. A calm mind helps the food settle better in your stomach."

Later, their bellies full, the two women relaxed beside the fire as the mountain night descended—the cold blackness of the sky relieved only by the crystal glitter of the stars. In the distance, a lone wolf raised its mournful howl. It was not answered.

Yrsa broke the silence that lay between them. "I feel like that wolf must, Eren. I call out to my husband—by name, by touch—and he doesn't answer me. I fear he can't." She began to weep, softly at first, then the tears came unrestrained.

An expression of compassion passed across Eren's face. "Tell me about it," she said softly.

Yrsa poured out the whole story to the elf-woman, who listened quietly and did not interrupt her visitor except to ask an occasional question. Her story told, Yrsa felt much better—she instinctively trusted Eren and perceived her to be a person of power. Surely the sympathetic norn would tell Yrsa that everything was going to be all right and that she need no longer worry.

Eren's first words hit her like a slap in the face and shattered her illusions. "Girl, do you have any idea what you are getting yourself into? Finding the dragon's lair isn't your problem—I'm pretty sure I know who he is and where he lives—but what do you think you are going to do when you get there? You have no experience with either weapons or magic, and I can assure you that the dragon will not yield up the sword just because you ask for it prettily."

"Well," said Yrsa hesitantly, "I thought you might tell me what to do."

Eren rolled her eyes skyward and muttered something under her breath about "Humans!" before responding somewhat brusquely: "The best advice I could give you would be to go home, accept your inevitable widowhood, and the next time pick a man who doesn't own a magic sword—but I'm sure you'd ignore me and get yourself killed anyway."

The elf-woman's voice softened as she saw the

shocked expression on Yrsa's face. "Besides, I know what it is to love so deeply that little else matters—including your own safety—when your beloved is in danger." Eren sighed. "Fact is, it was the death of Arvel, my fangmate, that caused me to flee Alfheim and become a norn. To behold the old familiar places without him beside me was just too painful to bear." She shook her head sadly. "So I *will* try to help you prepare for the ordeal—and hope that you survive it."

When Yrsa tried to express her gratitude, Eren cut her short with a curt retort. "Time enough to thank me when you come back from the dragon's lair." The unspoken ". . . if you do" hung in the air between them.

Eren patted Yrsa on the arm reassuringly. "The best thing you can do right now is to get a good night's sleep. You can spread your blankets on the birch boughs just inside the tent on the left. I'm going to sit up for awhile to ponder. We'll talk again in the morning."

Long after Yrsa had bidden the elf-woman a good night and closed the tent flap behind her, Eren sat by the dying embers of the fire, slowly sipping a cup of birch tea, and staring at the star called Odin's Eye, as if doing so might help her partake of the Allfather's vaunted wisdom —a wisdom that she and poor Yrsa sorely needed.

~

"Tell me, girl, who are you?" The challenge came shortly after Yrsa first awakened and sat up to stretch. Startled, she stammered, "Wh-why, I-I told you last night. I'm Yrsa Ivarsdotter, Princess of Ormerdal. Don't you remember?"

Eren waved aside the question impatiently. "You've

told me that you are your father's daughter and your husband's wife . . . but who is Yrsa herself? Who are you?" And she stared intently into Yrsa's eyes.

After a long moment's hesitation, Yrsa replied in a quavering voice, "I-I don't think I really know."

"Exactly," snapped Eren, "but you are going to have to find out before you can face the dragon. Your lineage has occasionally produced someone with a gift for magic—maybe, just maybe, you might be one of them. But even this hope will go for naught unless you find your *fylgja* and learn your true name."

"But I thought if a person saw his *fylgja* it meant that he was about to die," gasped Yrsa in dismay.

"And so it does for most people, girl, but one who has second-sight not only can see his 'companion' but can even talk to it. Are you willing to find out if you are one of those special people? Having such a gift can be as much a curse as a blessing, you know. As the saying goes, 'he who can see all is rarely happy.'"

"I don't really have much choice, do I," replied Yrsa, "but how do I go about finding my *fylgja*?"

"By going into the world where the fylgja dwells and letting it find you," remarked the elf-woman calmly. "If you are, indeed, one of the chosen ones, I can use the magic drum to separate your spirit from your body. Then your spirit will be free to seek its 'companion.'"

"But after my spirit finds the *fylgja*—if it does—will it be able to come back and rejoin my body? Will I ever be 'me' again?" asked Yrsa anxiously.

"If you have courage and remember that your *fylgja*—no matter in what form it may appear—is your guardian, and not your enemy, you should come to no harm, and your spirit will rejoin your physical body whenever you wish it to. But," Eren added solemnly, "you will never be the same 'you' again—and that is good. If there were no changes, you would have made the spirit journey for nothing. Now, if you are ready, we really should begin."

~

Yrsa lay naked upon her blankets and tried to relax as the soft but incessant beat of the magic drum filled the little tent. Against her will, Yrsa's mind filled to overflowing with questions, doubts, and fears. *What if I don't have the gift and can't go to the land of the fylgja? What if I do and can? Will I be able to come back again? If I do, what will I be like? Do I really want to do this? What am I doing here?* Then the faces of her beloved husband and her suffering subjects came into view and, with a leap of faith, she surrendered herself to the enchanting throb of the drum, which was coming to sound more and more like her own heartbeat. Mists swirled about her inner vision and, when they cleared, Yrsa seemed to be hovering near the top of the tent looking down upon her own recumbent form and the top of Eren's head as the elf-woman sat cross-legged, tapping rhythmically on the drumhead with a T-shaped antler beater.

For a moment, Yrsa felt a sense of confusion and vertigo, then—recognizing that she did, indeed, have the kind of power Eren had been talking about—she floated through the smokehole and rose high into the sky before soaring northward as Eren had instructed her to do. The sensation of flight was exhilerating, and Yrsa felt an identity with—and a deep bond of affection for—all the birds of the air, though, of course, none of those that she passed could see her or sense her presence.

Soon Yrsa spied the landmark she was seeking, a great dark fissure that lay between two ice-capped peaks, and she swiftly sank to earth. The walk up that narrow, rugged canyon seemed to take an eternity and yet but an instant—for what is time in the land where the *fylgja* dwells? Yrsa followed a sparkling rivulet until she reached the place where the two walls of the canyon came together and she could go no farther. There a small waterfall formed a shallow pool, which in turn fed the rivulet that had been her companion to this point, where she now sought another. On either side of the waterfall, at about head height, the walls of the canyon bore a series of angular red marks that Yrsa recognized as being runes, though she knew not their meanings.

Not knowing what she should do next, Yrsa stood quietly beside the pool, facing the waterfall and waiting for something to happen.

"I wondered if you were ever going to come," a warm, squeaky voice chittered as a sleek, furry brown head popped up out of the water almost at Yrsa's feet. "On the day you were born, the norns gave me the task of looking after you. When they told me you would be one of the gifted ones, I could hardly wait for you to come find me. But you never did," the otter-*fylgja* added reproachfully. "What were you waiting for?"

"I didn't know," said Yrsa quietly. "I never realized." Then as she began to comprehend what a unique bond of companionship her ignorance had kept from her all these lost years, Yrsa burst into tears.

"There, there, dear heart," the otter-*fylgja* said soothingly, "It's not as if I *really* blame you—'everything in its time,' as they say—it's just that we won't have the time to get acquainted slowly, the way it's supposed to happen when you're a child. Now we have no time for long romps in the pool—if you're to face that nasty dragon soon, you'll have to undergo the ritual of power as soon as I can instruct you."

"How do you know about the dragon?" Yrsa asked in astonishment. "We've only just met."

"*You've* only just met me; I've been with you since the day you were born. I've seen everything you have seen and know your every thought. Don't you understand yet? I am a part of you." The beast sat up in the shallows, its forepaws folded over its chest. "But whether you fully understand or not, we really must get started. Now, listen carefully to my words. The water in this pond is very special, for it comes from Hvergelmir, Mimir's Well, and Urd's Well; thus it contains the properties of all three— creativity, wisdom, and healing."

"But how can that be?" interrupted Yrsa. "Hvergelmir lies in Niflheim, Mimir's Well in Jötunheim, and Urd's Well in Asgard."

"Please be still and listen," admonished the otter-*fylgja*. "This is the water that drips from the World Tree, Yggdrasil. Since the Tree has roots in all three of those mighty springheads, any water that issues from Yggdrasil comes from them as well."

"Oh," said a somewhat chastened Yrsa, "I think I see."

"At last," sighed her *fylgja*. "Now, in order to come into your power, you must bathe beneath the waterfall. There, too, you will receive your true name. Fear not, and all shall be well." Yrsa did as she was told and waded through the pool to stand, arms uplifted, beneath the cascading water. At first the water seemed so cold that it almost took her breath away, but in just a few moments she began to feel as if a tongue of fire was burning away her flesh from head to foot. The girl felt an almost unbearable urge to scream and to stagger away from the source of her torment—but, trusting in her *fylgja's* promise, she stood fast and endured. Soon her pain faded away to be replaced with a sense of inner power, clear vision, and tranquility such as Yrsa had never before experienced. In that instant she knew, without asking, her true name.

Yrsa waded serenely toward the pool's edge, then paused and knelt down to retrieve a sparkling object that she spied at her feet. It was a large, glittering crystal, a scrying stone that would enable her to foresee future events—a powerful naming-gift, indeed, from the Norns, who ruled this place. Yrsa emerged from the pool to face the left-hand group of runes, which to her newly acquired vision glowed intensely and whose deepest meanings she now comprehended. Studying them intently for a few moments, she gave a little gasp of recognition and pleasure. Lightly placing her left hand on the G-rune, and her right hand on her own breast, she turned to her *fylgja* and said simply, "We are Gebo."

"I know," replied the beast softly. "And now you must return to your own world and face the dragon—but remember, you have only to open your mind to me and I'll be there with you."

~

Eren had been delighted at Yrsa's success and, after instructing her briefly but intensively on the uses of Yrsa's newly released power, had led her by twisting trails and

108   hidden paths to the verge of a deep ravine that fissured the southern slope of Rundhovd. There the elf-woman halted.

"I would go with you if I could, Yrsa, believe me. But it is your *wyrd* to face the dragon alone, and no one—not even a norn—can defy the power of *wyrd*."

Eren hugged Yrsa tightly, then released her. "Go now, and I pray that we shall see each other again." Tears gleamed in the elf-woman's eyes.

Yrsa, with a lump in her throat, turned silently and carefully began to scramble down the ravine wall, making use of every vine and rocky outcrop to secure a foothold or handhold. Once she had safely reached the bottom, Yrsa looked up and waved at the lonely figure of Eren on the ravine's rim.

It was getting late in the day and the depths of the ravine were in shadow as Yrsa made her way toward its head. At one point, she knelt to touch the water in the small stream that ran along the ravine floor and was astonished to find it was quite warm—surely there must be a hot spring at the source. Shortly thereafter, Yrsa turned a sharp bend and spied the entrance to a large cave and, sprawling on a broad ledge above the cave's mouth where it could bask in the last rays of the afternoon sun, an enormous dragon encased in gleaming blue-black scales.

Wait a minute, thought Yrsa, startled. *The dragon that stole the sword was silver, not blue . . . and smaller, too. This must be his mate.* Though Yrsa's grasp of dragon lore was fairly limited, she did recall hearing that mature females were always larger than the males. *Don't tell me I'm going to have to deal with two dragons!* Yrsa glanced quickly and apprehensively over her shoulder before remembering that after dragons mate the female chases the male away and broods the eggs alone. The shrunken abdomen of this female was a clear sign that she had recently laid eggs. *Guess they must be inside the cave,* Yrsa mused. *Well, even if I don't have to worry about the male, I'd better do something about this female before she wakes up and does something about me!*

Stepping into full view of the dragon, who now began to stir and raise her head, Yrsa began to sing softly and trace glowing runes in the air between them. "An ice-rune to slow you down and a bind-rune to hold you fast," murmured Yrsa.

The dragon's eyes snapped open and she tried to spew her venomous breath at the girl, but she was a split second too late. The runes had taken effect and all the dragon could manage was a poisonous sneeze.

"This-s-s will teach me, human," raged the immo-bilized dragon. "I s-s-sens-sed your approach from the moment you entered my ravine. . . but s-s-since you were a female and carried no iron, I thought you were no threat to me. Jus-st a careless-s-s, curious-s-s human wandering right up to my doors-step." She hissed in frustration. "I never s-s-sens-sed your rune power until you began to us-se it. It was-sn't you who was-s-s the careless-s-s, curious-s-s one, it was-s-s I. Now I s-s-suppos-se you will us-se your power to des-stroy me and my eggs-s-s."

When Yrsa remained silent, the dragon continued. "I have lived a long time and probably des-serve to be killed for my careless-sness-s-s. My only regret is-s-s that my offs-spring will never have a chance to grow up and experience the joys-s-s of dragonhood . . . to bas-sk in the s-s-sun, to ride the winds-s-s, and to mate well." What could only be a tear trickled down from the corner of her

110   gleaming, golden eye across her lower eyelid and fell to the ground.

Yrsa was totally nonplussed. She had heard that the greater orms were intelligent, but she had always considered them to be unfeeling monsters, aliens. The emotions being expressed by this mother dragon were disturbingly like those Yrsa knew she would feel under similar circumstances. Was there really so little difference between her and this hulking, scaly beast?

Logic told her that her safety and the success of her quest could best be assured by killing the dragon and destroying her eggs, but still Yrsa hesitated. This dragon and her brood had not harmed her or hers—nor, for that matter, had the male done so intentionally. As Yrsa debated with herself, a squeaky voice sounded in her mind: "Think well before you destroy that which you have not the power to create."

Yrsa smiled and straightened her shoulders, then stepped closer to the great she-dragon and told her of the misfortunes her silvery mate's theft of the sword had caused. "So you see, I don't wish to harm you or your eggs. I just want the sword back. Then I will happily leave you and your brood alone. If you will agree to that—and promise in your true name that there will be no revenge taken on me, my husband, or our realm—I'll go get the sword and nullify the runic charm when I leave."

"I would agree if I could, human, but the dragon code requires-s-s that we exact vengeance if anything is-s-s removed from our hoard by theft or duress-s-s. Even to s-s-save my young ones-s-s I cannot defy that law; it is-s-s writ in dragons-sblood on the Ormers-stein, which s-s-stands-s-s at the very brink of Hvergelmir. One might as-s-s eas-sily change the cours-se of the s-s-stars-s-s."

"What if I were to give you a gift?" queried Yrsa. "You know the old saying, 'a gift calls for a gift.' Well, then, you could give me the sword as a gift, and the dragon code wouldn't be broken, would it?"

"By the night-black s-s-scales-s-s of Nidhogg, I think you may have found the ans-swer," hissed the dragon. "But what gift can you give me that is-s-s of equal value to a magic s-s-sword? Balance is-s-s required, you know."

"Would you accept my naming gift?" asked Yrsa simply. "It is a scrying stone from the land where the *fylgja* dwells."

"A gift calls-s-s for a gift, indeed," remarked the dragon quietly. "You mus-st love your prince a great deal to give up s-s-so much for him. Yes-s-s, it is-s-s an acceptable gift. You may take the s-s-sword from my hoard. Jus-st put the crys-stal in its-s-s place. There will be no revenge taken; this-s-s I vow in my true name—Valdai."

"My true name is Gebo," offered the girl, not wanting to have the dragon at any further disadvantage. Then, following the small stream that issued from the cave's mouth, Yrsa passed beneath the dragon's ledge and entered the cave.

Beyond a short, dark passageway not much wider than Valdai's body, the cave opened into a broader cavern dimly lit by the glow of the dragon's golden hoard that nearly filled it. A hot spring bubbled forth from a crevice in the back wall, and its steaming water pooled beneath the lowermost level of the hoard before forming the stream that drained out through the ravine. Nested in a depression amidst the gold and silver nearer the top of the hoard were Valdai's eggs—nine of them—each the size of a human skull. Yrsa touched one gingerly and found the greenish-gray shell to be leathery, rather than hard and brittle like a bird's egg.

Yrsa's hand slipped accidentally and came to rest on the surface of the hoard. To her surprise, the metallic portions were warm to the touch. In that instant, Yrsa discovered a secret known to only a few masters of dragon lore—and one which they guard jealously—namely that the reason female dragons are drawn to a male's hoard is so they can provide adequate warmth for their developing eggs. Only the male who has chosen a cave with a good hot spring—yet provided it with a deep enough hoard to keep the eggs from being cooked—can hope to attract the most discriminating of females to his bower, thus ensuring both dragon "games" and healthy descendants.

The sword of Ormerdal had been thrust into the very top of the hoard, and Yrsa had some difficulty keeping her balance as she scrambled up the loose, shifting sides of the pile to retrieve it. With a long sigh of relief—but also with almost a sense of anticlimax—she claimed the blade and replaced it with her scrying stone. Gebo, whose name means "Gift" in the Old Tongue, had received a gift and had given it away again—for love.

Three days later, a travel-weary, but happy Yrsa—having released Valdai from her spell and paid a farewell visit to Eren—rode into Ormsby and up to the great hall where she and Solvenn lived. Great was the rejoicing at her return and, when she unwrapped the blanket-covered bundle she carried to reveal the missing sword, Yrsa was lifted aloft by the folk and carried on their shoulders to the prince's chamber. There she restored the sword to its scabbard, thus completing the ritual of kingship. The speedy recovery thereafter of both Solvenn and Ormerdal was little short of miraculous.

When the details of Yrsa's adventures came to be known, the skald Dag Ormseeker composed a song, "Yrsa's Deed," that soon spread throughout Ormerdal and beyond . . . and was always sung in Ormsby on the anniversary of her triumphant return. The words of the song went like this:

> *"Above, the watchful dragon waits,*
> *Scales glitt'ring in the sun;*
> *Beneath, the narrow portal frowns,*
> *A gauntlet to be run.*
>
> *Beyond the shadowed entranceway*
> *There lies her precious hoard;*
> *The gleam of gold and throbbing jewels,*
> *And best . . . a magic sword.*
>
> *Who'll stand and speak the proper rune,*
> *Keep dragon from the gate,*
> *And slip within the portal cleared*
> *To free the blade of fate?*
>
> *Only a maid by love empow'red,*
> *Reborn 'neath icy springs,*
> *Dare face drake fell to cast a spell*
> *And raise the sword of kings."*

Queen Yrsa and King Solvenn remained a devoted couple to the end of their days—which were many—and they ruled Ormerdal both wisely and well. Many folk noticed that Yrsa was changed somehow after her return from Rundhovd. She seemed older and more confident,

114   and increasingly Solvenn sought her counsel in matters of state. Her advice always proved sound and, in time, she came to gain quite a reputation as a wisewoman. As for Solvenn, though his people loved him dearly for his courage, compassion, and generosity, it was generally agreed that the wisest thing he had ever done was to marry Yrsa.

⌘

The Ragnarök Quartet

Ragnarök, the Doom of the Gods, hung over the Nine Worlds literally from their creation. Subsequent events led, slowly and inexorably, to that cataclysmic climax of the great mythic drama of the North; and in each of these stories, Ragnarök clearly was very much on the mind of the narrator. The opening narrative of the Ormseeker Cycle, "Theft of the Sun," could as easily have introduced this group of tales, since the events it relates foreshadow much that follows in the Ragnarök Quartet. Dag may well have learned of "The Courtship of Gerd" from Skirnir, but the last three stories were known only to the gods—until Odin's ravens, Hugin and Munin, passed them on to me.

⌘

The Courtship of Gerd

I misdoubted the whole affair from the very beginning. But when your status in the household of a god is that of a servant, your role is to carry out your lord's commands regardless of your own misgivings. And we elves are well known for keeping our opinions to ourselves; it adds to the aura of mystery that others perceive surrounding us.

Still I might have ventured to ask what was troubling my lord Frey, already deeply melancholy, had it not been likely to render him ill-tempered as well. We had practically grown up together, for I became his servant-companion as soon as he was old enough to need one, and it was only fitting that the overlord of Alfheim be served by an elf-chief's son. In all the ensuing years I had not seen Frey in such a state, so I concluded that discretion was the better part of valor, at least until he indicated a desire to talk.

Alas, my discretion was not a luxury I was to enjoy for long Frey's refusal to eat or drink, as well as his all-pervasive moodiness, soon came to the attention of his father, Njörd. I don't know if Njörd tried to speak with Frey and failed, or if the old fellow just didn't feel comfortable enough about having a father-son talk even to try. In any event, early one morning Njörd summoned me into his presence and, having determined that I didn't know what ailed his "boy," ordered me to find out. I respectfully expressed my doubts about encountering anything more than an angry outburst, but Njörd was adamant; so I could demur no further, and I agreed to do as he bade me.

~

"Frey, my friend, what ails you so?" I queried after my soft knock on the door of his bed-closet drew a terse "Go away!"

"I don't want to talk about it," Frey muttered—and the door remained closed.

Presuming on our long friendship, I persisted. "Frey, we've known each other since boyhood and have always shared everything, the bad times as well as the good. You've got to talk to someone about your troubles, or you're just going to fade away. Won't you let me help you?"

The door to the bed-closet slowly swung open, and Frey sat up on the edge of his bed. "I guess you're right, Skirnir, but I feel so miserable that I'm no fit company for anyone. I can't eat and I can't sleep for thinking about her." He pushed back his shock of golden hair with both hands.

Her? I pounced on the word. "What 'her' are you talking about . . . and why should the very thought of her be making you sick?"

"Oh, Skirnir, I'm in love! I'm in love with Gerd Gymirsdatter." And Frey sighed deeply.

"Gymir the Hill Giant?" I intoned the name incredulously. "When did all this happen? I didn't think you'd visited Jötunheim in years."

"I haven't, but I saw her in a vision from Hlidskjalf. She had just stepped out of the door of her father's hall and held out her arms as if greeting the day. So white were her shining arms, they lit the sky and sea. Could any woman be more beautiful?"

"She certainly sounds lovely, the way you describe her. But, by all that's holy, my lord, whatever possessed you to sit on Odin's high throne? You know that the All-Father has forbidden that privilege to any save himself. Disaster is sure to follow this act."

"It already has, Skirnir, it already has. No punishment that Odin could mete out would make me feel worse than I already do. If I can't have Gerd as my wife, I'll die. I mean that with all my heart, Skirnir. Life just wouldn't be worth living without her." Frey paused. "I wonder if Loki knew what was going to happen when he encouraged me to sit on Hlidskjalf—'Go ahead and do it, Frey, nobody will ever know,' he said."

"Loki talked you into this foolishness?" I was

horrified. "Oh, Frey, how could you have trusted any-thing that sly fox said? You know he loves nothing better than to cause discord among the gods."

"I know, I know. But a part of me was curious about what Odin can see from his throne, so it didn't take too much persuasion to convince me." Frey sighed. "Still, my foolishness and Loki's malice aside, the fact remains that I sat, I saw, and I was smitten. You did say you wanted to help me, my friend?"

"I did, my lord, and I still do. But how?" I replied, perplexed.

"Go to Jötunheim, to Gymir's steading, and win the bright-armed maiden for me. I told you I can't live without her." Frey's eyes met mine pleadingly.

"But surely you could court her better yourself. Why would you want me to go?" That I found the prospect distasteful my voice undoubtedly betrayed.

"The gods are sure to disapprove of such a marriage and would stop me from going. And the giants consider me an enemy, so bloodshed would ensue long before we could get around to talk of wooing and wedding. The gods pay little attention to your comings and goings, and the giants wouldn't see you as a threat. You would be the ideal messenger to plead my cause." When I hesitated, he went on, "Please say you'll do this for me—if you're successful, I'll reward you beyond your wildest dreams." Frey held out both arms in supplication.

"Gold and jewels weigh but little when friendship is in the balance, my lord," I replied somewhat stiffly, offended that Frey might think he needed to buy my loyalty. "But I will ask for the loan of your horse and your sword—the one that fights giants by itself—that I might defend myself if the wooing goes badly and Gymir becomes violent."

Frey grasped my forearms excitedly. "Then you'll go, Skirnir? I knew I could count on you. Bloody Hoof and my sword are at your disposal . . . and anything else you need. Can you leave at once?"

His excitement thawed me. "As soon as Bloody Hoof can be saddled, and I can pack my saddlebags, we'll be on our way."

"Thank you again, best of friends. And with my life in the balance, I know you won't take 'No' for an answer—from either Gerd or her father."

"Fear not, Frey . . . I won't."

~

The ride through the misty mountains to Jötunheim was uneventful enough until Bloody Hoof and I drew near to Gymir's steading, where a flickering glow caught my eye. At first I thought that Gymir's hall itself was ablaze, but when I came within sight of my goal I saw that the entire steading was barred to the outer world by a wall of flame—save for a towering stone gateway opposite the hall. But there would be no easy access through that portal, for chained to either side of the gateway was a savage hound that growled fiercely and strained at its binding when it caught sight of my horse and me.

I reined in Bloody Hoof and, espying a shepherd sitting beneath a nearby tree, inquired: "Tell me, good fellow, how is one supposed to get past those hounds to reach Gymir's hall? I have come a long way to speak with his daughter, Gerd."

The herdsman was silent for a moment, sucking his

lip pensively. Then, with something approaching a twinkle in his rheumy eyes, he replied: "Weel, yew see, sor, thet's sorta the point, ain't it? Strangers—lak yew, beggin' yer pardon, I'm sure—ain't supposed ter get past them dawgs. Thet's why Gymir put them thar, 'tis. Turrible feerce they be, too, sor. 'Twould hate ter see yew and yer nice horsie all torn ter leetle bits. Messy, thet would be." He shook his shaggy, grey head slowly and sorrowfully. "Best yew turn about now, sor, and go back home . . . whilst yew can."

I shrugged, without visible emotion, and responded: "One's *wyrd* alone determines what is possible and what is not. One thing I do know—faint heart never knows good luck."

With that I leaned forward, whispered into Bloody Hoof's ear, and we charged forward—but not at the gateway and its ferocious guardians. No, we headed directly at the wall of fire and, at what I sensed to be just the critical moment, I tapped the horse's flank and flattened myself against his neck. Bloody Hoof responded by leaping as high and as far through the flames as his stout heart and powerful legs would carry him. And as *wyrd* would have it—though the heat was nigh unto unbearable—neither the horse nor I was harmed.

Thwarted in their role as guardians of the gateway, the two hounds set up an awful howl. Gerd must have heard the commotion from within the hall, for shortly— as I allowed Bloody Hoof to graze on the grass—a serving maid stuck her head out the door to see what was going on. She stared at me, open-mouthed, for a moment, then disappeared back into the hall. Soon Gerd herself appeared, and I must admit that, despite his being lovesick, Frey had not exaggerated her beauty. Being a giantess, Gerd was much bigger-boned than would normally appeal to elvish tastes, but she certainly was a magnificent-looking woman!

This impression was only reinforced when she spoke, for she had a warm, throaty voice. "Who are you, stranger? Are you one of the Aesir, a Van, or perhaps an elf?"

"I am Skirnir the elf, fair lady, but I come on behalf of one of the Vanir. My master, Lord Frey, has loved you from afar and wishes to marry you."

"Me, marry one of the gods? Why would I ever want to do that?" Gerd asked incredulously.

"Perhaps my lady would consider Idunn's golden apples of eternal youth a sufficient inducement," I offered.

"I *have* youth and beauty . . . what need have I for Idunn's silly apples?" she retorted.

"Well, one can never have enough gold," I countered. "Would Odin's magic ring, Draupnir, which produces eight gold rings every ninth night, stir your heart?"

"My father's treasure room contains all the gold I could ever need," Gerd replied haughtily.

By the red beard of Thor, beauty or not, this giantess was stubborn beyond belief and arrogant to boot! She seemed to have no notion of the great honor Frey was offering her. Having to bargain with her like a fishmonger was galling, yet Frey had admonished me not to take "No" for an answer, and so far that was all I had heard from Gerd. Normally elves are the very soul of patience— and the thought of coercing another being is abhorrent to us—but with Frey pining away and me having the responsibility to save him, I'm afraid I violated the Alfar code.

For which there'll be a price to pay, I'm sure.

"Beware of overweening pride, lady. Do you see this sword?" And I half drew Frey's blade from its scabbard.

"What is that sword to me? Are . . . are you *threatening* me with it?" Gerd stared at me as if the very idea was too ridiculous to be believed.

"Indeed, I am," I replied coldly and with as much dignity as I could muster. "Unless you agree to marry Lord Frey, I am going to smite your head from your body."

Folding her arms and cocking her head, she considered me skeptically. "Neither my head nor my body would be of much use to your master if they were separated, would they? No, Skirnir, your threat is an empty one."

Curse the woman, she was shrewder than I'd anticipated. Curse the woman? Ah ha, that might be the answer. If the final death held no fear for her, perhaps a living death might. That an elf would even consider such a thing reveals how desperate I had become. Extracting a flat, narrow birch wand from my saddlebag, I drew my belt knife and began to carve a series of arcane symbols on the flattened surface.

Gerd eyed my actions suspiciously and finally asked: "Tell me, Skirnir, what *are* you up to?"

"You have tried my patience too far, lady," I replied. "Do you see this wand I hold in my hand? I have scratched four curse runes upon it—one each for loathing, lust, trolls, and filth. If you do not agree at once to marry Frey, I will invoke these curses upon your head. Would you hear what they are?"

Warily, Gerd nodded and silently awaited my proclamation.

"Well, then," I began, "should I invoke these

curses, you shall be condemned to sit alone on a barren mountain peak facing Hel's Gate, barely able to swallow food that will have become as loathsome to you as a slithery knot of serpents. Your comely face shall become so repulsive that everyone will avoid your company, and you shall be plagued with unbearable sadness and constant weeping. Should you visit the Frost Giants, their wee ones will pursue you, pinching and pulling, all the day long as—bent and broken in body—you hobble about the hall."

I paused for breath, and to judge the impact on Gerd of what I had said. Her fists were clenched, her lips parted, and worry lines had appeared at the corners of her deep blue eyes, so I went on.

"Odin and Thor, and even Frey, shall be furious with you, all three tribes of giants shall despise you, and the joy and love of men shall be denied you. You shall be wracked with overwhelming lust, yet none shall agree to marry you save an ugly three-headed troll! That's right, you'll be forced to mate with gruesome old Hrimgrimnir in the bowels of Niflheim where, in a dim grotto beneath the root of the Tree, drooling slaves shall serve you goat urine—the only drink you shall ever have again."

Gerd shuddered and gulped. A part of me was ashamed of what I was putting her through, but I steeled myself to complete the task.

"Now is the moment of decision, lady. If you would stay the curses, agree to be Frey's wife, and I will scrape the wood clean of the runes. If you will not, I have but to say one word and the curses will begin their work. Once said, that word cannot be taken back, and no power in the Nine Worlds can overturn the curses it sets in motion." I wasn't altogether certain that my last statement was completely true, but I doubted if Gerd would know that.

Gerd raised the palms of her hands in surrender and swallowed hard. "Enough, Skirnir, enough. I yield to your threats, and I shall marry your master . . . though what happiness for either of us can grow out of such a courtship, I know not."

Turning toward the hall, Gerd clapped her hands to fetch her serving maid, who made such a rapid appearance that she surely must have been eavesdropping from just within the portal. Her mistress sent her off on an errand, and shortly the maid returned bearing a crystal goblet filled with golden mead. After sipping from one side of the cup, Gerd held it out to me with these words: "With this cup, I pledge myself to wed Frey. Drink you now, Skirnir, as his spokesman, to seal the pledge."

"With all my heart, Lady Gerd." I downed the rest of the drink and handed the goblet to the serving maid. "Now tell me—for Lord Frey is sure to ask—just when and where the marriage shall take place?"

Gerd sighed: "Tell Frey that I will meet him at the trysting glade in the forest of Barri nine nights hence. There shall we be wed."

I bowed to her and remounted Bloody Hoof for my ride home. As I passed through the gateway—the hounds having since been tethered on short chains—I looked back and extended my arm in salute to a brave and noble lady.

Gerd waved back and called out: "My father will send word of the bride-price before the wedding. Farewell, Skirnir."

~

Of the long ride back, there is little to say. No sooner had I come in sight of Frey's abode than he rushed out to greet me and demand news of my mission.

"Skirnir, Skirnir, what news have you for me? Will Gerd marry me?"

After I had dismounted and handed Bloody Hoof's reins to a stable boy, I replied: "She will, indeed, my lord —nine nights hence in the forest of Barri."

Frey's mouth gaped. "Nine nights? One night without her seems like a year, two an eternity. How can I possibly wait for nine?"

~

But he did, and the wedding took place as planned. And, as time passes, Gerd even seems to be happy being Frey's wife. He, of course, is beside himself with joy.

Then why do I continue to have misgivings? Well, remember the bride-price? When Gymir sent his message, he demanded Frey's sword as Gerd's bride-price. He said it would be a token of good faith on Frey's part; after all, if Frey was going to marry a giantess, why would he need a sword that slew giants by itself—that would hardly be a friendly way to treat his new wife's kinfolk!

Gymir's argument sounds reasonable on the surface—and Frey wanted Gerd so badly he would have given her father his right arm if he'd asked for it—but giants *are* giants, and that sword was second only to Thor's hammer as a defense against an invasion from Jötunheim. Now the sword is gone. I can't speak for others in Asgard, but I sleep much less easily these nights.

⌘

Freyja's Tears

"Why must you go, Od?" Freyja's voice was plaintive as, hugging her knees, she sat up on the bearskin rug where they had spent the night. Her golden hair, usually braided, hung free—partially framing, yet partially concealing, her lovely face. Her rosy cheeks were pale now and her light blue eyes glistened with barely suppressed tears. "We've been together less than a fortnight. Surely you have not tired of me already?"

Odin's voice was tender as he tied the drawstring of

his trousers and prepared to pull the tunic over his broad, bare torso, unmarked save for a long spear-scar lying beneath his ribcage. "It has been nine days and nights, dearest Freyja, and each of them has been precious to me. So different from the nine I spent upon the Tree, seeking the knowledge of the runes—nothing then but the cold wind, driving rain, gnawing hunger, and unutterable loneliness . . . yet, in the end, I found that which I had sought," he added grimly. "Here with you there has been nothing but joy, yet I have gained great knowledge as well—though it has come unbidden. In your blue eyes there are greater deeps and more wondrous mysteries than any my lost eye beheld in Mimir's Well."

Freyja rose to her feet and softly kissed the lidded socket that once contained the price Mimir had demanded for a single draught from the Well of Wisdom. "Poor, dear man," she murmured. Odin embraced her lithe golden-tan form like a drowning man clasps a fortune-brought tree trunk drifting by. Holding her thus he could sense her inner being, which reflected the essence of the living, fertile earth—all browns, and greens, and gold.

"You aren't going to make this easy for me, are you?" he whispered huskily in her ear. "Listen well, my love. Had I a choice, we would never part for so much as a day. Over the years I have loved many a maid, and loved each of them truly—even poor Gunnlöd, though 'twas my intention at first just to trick her into letting me drink the Mead of Poetry she guarded 'neath Suttung's gloomy mountain . . . but then her loneliness touched my heart."

Odin sighed and rubbed his grizzled beard. "But none have I loved as I love you. There are times when you fill my soul like a bracing wind sweeping down off a glacier, and I could cry out for the sheer exhilaration of being alive. At other times, holding your hand in silence, I can feel the gentle rhythms that ebb and flow throughout the Nine Worlds—and I am content with the stillness. Moreover, you have helped me find the one thing that the runes could not, and the waters of Mimir's Well could not, and the Mead of Poetry could not. You have helped me to find myself. Whenever I look into your eyes or hold you in my arms, I forget that I am Odin Allfather, King of the Gods, Ruler of the Nine Worlds, whom all respect, fear, or hate because of my power."

Odin's voice shook with exhultation, "All I see is an ordinary, weather-beaten old man who is himself—nothing more, nor less—and who is loved by Freyja. What greater knowledge does one need, or better fortune hope to gain? Though," he added ruefully, "it is quite beyond my comprehension what a beautiful woman like you—who is neither awed by my power nor seeking my favor—sees in an old gaffer like me."

"Oh, Od," she laughed throatily. "There really are some things you don't understand for all of your hard-earned wisdom. You can look beyond my outer appearance—though not entirely, I'm happy to say—" and she grinned mischievously, "so why shouldn't I be able to do likewise? I love you for your boyish curiosity as much as for your mature wisdom, for your gentle compassion as much as for your fierce strength, and for reasons that even I don't fully understand. Besides, I think it is wiser to simply accept and enjoy our love rather than question the 'why' of it." Freyja frowned. "Anyway, if my love means so much to you, why must you leave me now and cause us both so much pain?"

Odin pulled his dark blue traveling cloak around

130   his shoulders and secured it with an enamelled dragon brooch. "It is because I do love you so much, darling Freyja, that I must go. In your arms I can forget my cares and responsibilities for a time, but they are a burden I cannot lay aside for long lest the Nine Worlds suffer— including our own homeland, fabled Asgard. I fear that Loki or the giants would do some mighty mischief if I did not keep a close eye on them. The giants fear me, and I must keep that fear alive by appearing among them from time to time just so they don't start to wonder if I haven't forgotten them. Even the thought that I might be wandering about in disguise helps to curb their ambitions."

Odin paused, pensive. "And I must watch the warriors of Midgard, too, to see which promising heroes are worthy of joining the ranks of the Einherjar in Valhalla. When Ragnarök comes, and the forces of Order and Chaos clash, we must have the best army I can assemble—we must!"

Freyja bowed her head in sad resignation as Odin placed his hands on her shoulders and said, "So you see, beloved, why I cannot tarry here. But know with a certainty that I shall return to you whenever I can." Freyja's shoulders shook as she sobbed quietly, and Odin continued. "Now I will leave you with something tangible to serve as a symbol of my pledge. Henceforth, when you cry for me, your tears will turn into drops of gold. When enough have fallen, carry them to those dwarves whom men call the Brisings and they will fashion a necklace for you. Whene'er you wear it, you will think of me and know that a part of us can never truly be separated."

Taking Freyja's face in his hands and closing each eyelid with a forefinger, Odin gifted her with a poem:

"Though space and time forbid our touch,
I hold thee close within my heart;
And while I wander far from thee,
My feet tread gently through thy soul."

Lightly tracing a love rune on each of her eyelids, Odin kissed them in turn, then stepping back he simply disappeared. Not a sound followed his abrupt departure, save for Freyja's quiet sobbing—and a muted clinking as a pile of golden tears slowly grew upon the rug at her feet.

⌘

Loki Bound

"Hurry, woman, hurry!"

The scream is torn from my lips despite my determination not to acknowledge the pain—the excruciating pain—that wracks my face and chest every time the bowl fills with venom and Sigyn has to leave the cave to empty it. If she poured it out in here, the venom would run down into the hot springs, and the fumes would kill her. Her, not me—oh, no, not me. The Aesir are too clever by far to let me have that easy a death. They know, Hel rot them, that serpent venom can't kill me—just burn with the searing pain of ice. Not like fire. They know I like fire, even if they don't know why. Oh, gods, why doesn't Sigyn hurry? The venom can't kill me, but the pain may drive me mad. No, I can't let it. I've got to endure the pain so I can avenge myself on them . . . starting with that icy bitch Skadi who came up with the idea of fastening that drooling serpent over my head. A nice touch, I'll give her that . . . and a lot more when I get loose. And I will get loose—I've just got to be patient.

"Oh, that feels so much better, Sigyn." She has reseated herself by my side, wifely concern etched in every feature. "Could you rinse the venom from my face before the bowl becomes too full to hold in one hand? Thank you, my dear one, thank you. I don't know what I'd ever do without you."

I'll tell you what I would have done without her! If I'd never planted those two boys in her skinny body, the Aesir wouldn't have been able to fasten me to these rocks. Odin knew I could only be bound by the guts of one son, torn from his living body by his brother; and he certainly would never have gotten my other sons, Fenris Wolf and the World Serpent, to try to gut each other. Oh, my, no. That Fenris will be the death of Odin yet . . . when he gets loose, and that won't be long after me. Fenris and Jörmungand are really sons to be proud of! And their mother, Angrboda—oh, she was something to behold, too. A troll-wife might not be for the fastidious, but making love to her was always an adventure—she was always so eager to couple, and I never knew what my seed would grow into. Something different every time—the Wolf, the Serpent, and my darling daughter, Hel . . . with my handsome features on one side of her face, and her mother's on the other. Poor Sigyn, she has no idea how boring she and her brood have been by comparison. It's fortunate, though, that she is so devoted, considering the way things have turned out.

"What's that? Yes, Sigyn, I think Odin Allfather is being cruel and unreasonable, too. After all, it's not as if I cast the mistletoe dart at Balder all by myself. The Aesir are the ones who insisted on making him a target just to show off the invulnerability Mother Frigg had gained for him—or thought she had. There's an old saying: 'Pride rarely sees the pitfall in the path,' and the Aesir were just aching to be taught a lesson."

Actually, I hadn't disliked Balder all that much personally. He never really approved of any of my pranks—I could see that by the disdainful looks he'd give me. But he wasn't a bully like Thor or a busybody like Heimdall. Heimdall! If it hadn't been for him I would have hidden Freyja's necklace where she never would have found it . . . until she was willing to pay my price. Why should Heimdall have cared? I only wanted what those four dwarves wanted—and got—for selling the Brisingamen to her in the first place, a night of love-making with the most beautiful goddess in the Nine Worlds! Umm . . . just the thought of her shapely white body makes me drool. If Heimdall had wanted her for himself, that I could understand; but, no, he said he was simply "defending the honor of a dear friend." Honor, her? I still don't know if he is the biggest hypocrite in the Nine Worlds or just the most simple-minded. Either way, I've a score to settle with him, too.

But even Heimdall's interference wasn't as bad as what Odin has done to me. He and I swore sacred oaths of blood brotherhood, yet every time I did something that annoyed him he threatened to have me killed. That is why Balder had to die. Odin had to pay the price for oath-breaking, a price that really hurt—and his beloved son Balder was the most vulnerable. Too bad for Balder, but justice had to be served. Unfortunately, Odin wasn't willing to call it even at that . . . no, not him! He always has to have the last word or strike the last blow.

"Aieee . . . ! Sigyn, for pity's sake, be more careful, won't you? Yes, yes, I know it must be exhausting to hold that bowl steady, but you've no idea how painful a drop of that venom can be—especially when I'm not expecting it. There, there, my dear, don't cry about it—but do try not to let it happen again." I have to humor the clumsy cow; it wouldn't do to have her walk out on me now.

So here I lie in this god-forsaken cave to be tormented for all eternity . . . or so Allfather thinks. But Odin, you old bastard, you don't know everything after all. You don't even know who I really am. Oh, I admitted to being of giant stock right from the beginning, but that was just acknowledging the obvious to keep you from looking deeper. My parents are giants, all right, but not the Hill Giants Farbauti and Laufey, as I led you to believe. I am only their foster-son. My true birthplace was Muspellheim, the Flaming Land; my father, Surt the Destroyer, Lord of the Fire Giants; my mother, his lady, Sinmara. Surt wished to keep an eye on you Aesir; what better way than to have his son live in your midst? Father has bided his time 'til now, Odin, but by what you have done to me you have brought your doom down upon your head! Even now his hosts are gathering and, once Fenris Wolf and I have been freed, the Sons of Muspell will march across the Rainbow Bridge into Asgard. Then will come Ragnarök, the Doom of the Gods . . . and, after the Final Battle, Surt will turn the Nine Worlds to ashes with his flaming sword. But you won't see that will you, Odin, from the depths of Fenris's belly?

What's that Allfather? You think you are safe because nothing in the Nine Worlds can sunder my bonds and those that hold Fenris? Know then to your sorrow that after you exiled my daughter, Hel, to Niflheim, I paid

136 her an extended visit—but not entirely out of parental concern and devotion. You should know me better than that, once sworn-brother. No, I retired to a grotto beneath Niflheim, and there forged a sword . . . a very special sword to which the dead of Niflheim contributed certain key ingredients, liberally if not entirely voluntarily. I cast some mighty runes and sealed them into the blade with my own blood—the royal blood of Muspellheim. And when I was through, I held up Laevatein, the one rune-sword that can cut through any bonds, no matter how strong or magically well wrought.

Mother has kept Laevatein safe in a chest beneath her bed for just such a time as this. That chest is sealed against intruders with nine locks, and only one can be opened each day. That's right, Odin, just nine days from when you bound me here Sinmara will bring Laevatein to free me—and then my son Fenris.

"How long have I lain here, Sigyn? Nine days, did you say, my love?"

Across the Nine Worlds I can hear Sinmara coming. Do you hear her, too, Odin? It is the sound of Ragnarök approaching . . . .

⌘

Shadow of the Wolf

"Come, Hugin and Munin. Come, my ravens, come sit on my shoulders while I rest a bit before Fenris Wolf finds me. He won't be long, I'm sure, and I want to cling to Thought and Memory while I still can.

"When did it all start to go wrong? When did Order start to slide into Chaos? I thought that my brothers and I had created a perfect universe, the Nine Worlds, tied together and supported by Yggdrasil, the World Tree. Why did the giants become so hostile? Why couldn't they have been content with their own lands and their own women? Why did they always want ours? Is Ragnarök their fault? It would be easy to blame them for all our troubles, but wise Uncle Mimir's head advised me to look

closer to home. Is it possible—just remotely possible—
that our slaughtering the first giant, Ymir the Sleeper, to
obtain the matter from which we created the Nine Worlds
tainted the whole process from its very beginning? I've
started to wonder if anything begun in violence can come
to aught but a violent end.

"Many's the time I've regretted the way I treated
Gullveig when she overstayed her welcome in Asgard—
her incessant prattling about gold was beginning to plant
the seed of gold lust among my people. I could have
simply sent Gullveig back to her home in Vanaheim, but
I was so angry that I ordered her spitted and roasted.
Then, not only did the witch survive her intended
execution, but when the Vanir learned how we had
treated one of their own, they declared war on Asgard.
That turned out to be a very devastating, costly war—
and, to make matters worse, we lost! If the Vanir hadn't
decided to be merciful at the last, that could well have
been the end of Asgard and, perhaps, even the Aesir. And
all because I let Gullveig provoke me to violence.

"But I'm not the only one of the Aesir that's guilty
of that mistake, my friends. No, now that I reflect on it, I
can see that the deeds of my oldest son, Thor, have won
us no friends in Giant Home. Defending Asgard against
their raids was only right and proper, but the grisly after-
math of Thor's "hunting trips" into Jötunheim must have
given rise to many a bitter and implacable foeman. As for
his personal nemesis, Jörmungand the World Serpent, I'm
afraid that Thor created that enemy, too. While I merely
banished Jörmungand into the ocean when he grew too
large to live in Asgard any longer, Thor sought him out to
slay him. And today he has succeeded; Jörmungand is
dead—but so, too, is Thor, overcome by the Serpent's

venomous breath.

"So many deaths, and so many yet to come. Loki's scheming to bring about the death of my beloved son Balder with that cursed twig of mistletoe really set in motion the events that have led to this day. Loki, Loki . . . how could you have done it? We had been blood brothers—closer than kin. What ever could I have done to make you want to hurt me so? And now you, too, are gone—slain by Heimdall even as you killed him. Was your revenge worth it, Loki?

"And what of Frey, the light-hearted Lord of Alfheim and brother of my beloved Freyja? Alas, no more gaiety or laughter shall pass his now silent lips. To stand against Surt and his flaming sword with naught but a hart's antler was sheer futility, but poor, heroic Frey had no choice, for he had given up his giant-slaying sword as the bride-price for his giantess wife, Gerd. And now there is none to stop that mad Fire Giant from burning everything in sight—field and forest, friend and foe alike. Look! Listen! Smell! That flickering orange glow, those crackling sounds, and the odor of burning flesh mark his path.

"Alas, alas, my ravens, that everything my hands have touched should come to this! The Völva, that long-dead seeress, warned me this would happen when I summoned her from her eternal rest to tell me of Balder's fate. I believed what she prophesied then, and I see the truth of her vision played out before me now. But what could I have done differently? By then the Norns' tapestry was far too tightly woven to seek to unravel it and weave a new design. 'No man can avoid his *wyrd*,' they say—and no god, either, it seems.

"And now Fenris Wolf draws near. You can see his giant shadow cast by the flickering flames. He hates me for tricking and binding him—and I can't really blame him—but what else could I have done, waited until he had eaten one of us? And yet, and yet . . . in acting so drastically, so irrevocably, before the Wolf had actually given me any reason to do so—beyond his mere existence—did I not create my own nemesis as much as did my son Thor with the World Serpent?

"We'll never know, will we, my friends, for the consequences of the path I chose—of all the paths I have chosen—are bearing down upon me here today . . . now.

"So fly, Hugin; fly, Munin. Fly, Thought and Memory. And if you should survive Ragnarök, seek out the other survivors, gods and humans alike, and share my story—my thoughts and memories—with them. Give them my love . . . and tell them to weave the new strands of their *wyrd* with great care. They will be free to do that, you know, for the Norns' old loom is burning, too, and the Age to come will be the survivors' to create as they choose. Knowing this, I can die content. So fly with my blessing, faithful friends—you served me well, indeed.

"They're gone now, my Thought and Memory, and I'm left like many another old man awaiting his end. Hark, the shadow grows larger . . . and larger still. My doom is upon me, but I'll face it on my feet with my head unbowed. Come, Fenris, come. Odin fears you not!"

⌘

Epilogue

And so the cycles continue, for as the **ørlög** tells us when the Norns chant it each morning while applying the healing paste to the World Tree:

In the midst of darkness, light;
In the midst of death, life;
In the midst of chaos, order.

In the midst of order, chaos;
In the midst of life, death;
In the midst of light, darkness.

Thus has it always been,
Thus is it now, and
Thus shall it always be.

About Douglas "Dag" Rossman

Known for his spirited retellings of Norse myths and Viking tales, "Dag" Rossman is a gifted storyteller who shares a passion for Norse mythology with his wife Sharon, an artist. Dag's stories, most of them set in the Nine Worlds of Norse mythology, have appeared in the Sons of Norway's *Viking* magazine and *Mythic Circle* magazine. He wrote and she illustrated **The Nine Worlds: A Dictionary of Norse Mythology** (2000, Skandisk, Inc., Minneapolis, MN), and the two of them co-authored **Valhalla in America: Norse Myths in Wood at Rock Island State Park, Wisconsin** (1999, Jackson Harbor Press, Washington Island, WI). Dag's storytelling skills are in great demand at folk festivals, heritage camps, and other Scandinavian events. Five of his storytelling collections have been released by Skandisk, Inc. on audio-cassette (available in Scandinavian gift stores nationwide, or by calling 1-800-468-2424).

A biology professor at Louisiana State University for more than 35 years, "Dag" and his wife Sharon now live in Decorah, Iowa, where they served as guest curators for the Vesterheim Norwegian-American Museum's major exhibition "Echoes of Odin: Norse Mythology in Scandinavia and America."

⌘

Books and Tapes by "Dag" Rossman available from Skandisk, Inc.:

The Nine Worlds
A Dictionary of Norse Mythology
by Dag Rossman.
Illustrations by Sharon Rossman.

An annotated dictionary of the principal mythological beings, places, and magical implements mentioned in the *Eddas*—tales of Viking-age Scandinavia.
Paperback, 112 pp, $8.95;
ISBN 1-57534-014-3
LIT 320

Nordic legends on audiocassette...

Many of Dag Rossman's tales from Nordic mythology and Viking lore are available on audiocassette—perfect for listening to in the car! In *Troll Tales*, Rossman provides the background and history of trolls, and tells a number of troll stories. *Ice & Fire* is one of two cassettes of tales from Norse mythology. It focuses on Norse myths about the origin of the world. *Hammer & Mistletoe* contains stories about the adventures of Thor, the God of Thunder. Dating back to the Viking age, *The Ring of Doom* is the story of Sigurd the Dragon-Slayer and his ill-fated love for the valkyrie Brynhild. All Ages. **Audio Cassettes, $10.95 each.**

Hammer & Mistletoe
(90 minutes)
MCS 4840

The Ring of Doom
(60 minutes)
MCS 4860

Troll Tales
(52 minutes)
MCS 4850

Ice & Fire (90 minutes)
MCS 4835

NEW

Wizard Ways
Tales told by "Dag" Rossman

This latest collection of tales by acclaimed storyteller "Dag" Rossman will have you sitting on the edge of your seat as you follow these four adventures of Viking-age wizards. Lovers of fantasy will also be enchanted by these original Norse myths. All Ages. (55 minutes) **MCS 4870**

To order call: 1-800-468-2424